THE SEER

LINDA JOY SINGLETON lives in northern California. She has two grown children and a wonderfully supportive husband who loves to travel with her in search of unusual stories.

Linda Joy Singleton is the author of more than twenty-five books, including the series *Regeneration*, *My Sister the Ghost*, *Cheer Squad*, and, also from Llewellyn, *Strange Encounters*.

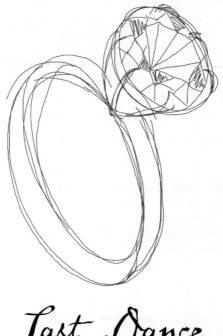

Last Dance

LINDA JOY SINGLETON

Llewellyn Publications
Woodbury, Minnesota

First Edition
Third Printing, 2007

Cover design and ring illustration by Lisa Novak
Editing by Rhiannon Ross

Library of Congress Cataloging-in-Publication Data
Singleton, Linda Joy.
    Last Dance/Linda Joy Singleton.—1st Llewellyn Edition
        p. cm.—(The Seer; #2)
    Summary: While trying to help her sick grandmother, Sabine and her Goth friend Thorn travel to a small California town where they become involved in a ghostly, fifty-year-old mystery.
    ISBN 0-7387-0638-8
    [1. Ghosts--Fiction. 2. Psychic ability--Fiction. 3. Supernatural--Fiction. 4. Grandmothers--Fiction. 5. California--Fiction] I. Title.
PZ7.S6177Las200
[Fic]--dc22
ISBN-13: 978-0-7387-0638-2

Llewellyn Publications
A Division of Llewellyn Worldwide, Ltd.
Llewellyn is a registered trademark of Llewellyn Worldwide, Ltd.
2143 Wooddale Drive, Dept. 0-7387-0526-8
Woodbury, MN 55125-2989, U.S.A.
www.llewellyn.com

Printed in the United States of America

Other Books in the Seer Series

The Seer #1, *Don't Die, Dragonfly*
The Seer #3, *Witch Ball*
The Seer #4, *Sword Play*

Coming soon from Linda Joy Singleton

The Seer #5, *Fatal Charm*

This book is dedicated to the memory of four talented and wonderful friends whom I miss and will never forget:

Dona Vaughn (author of *Chasing the Comet*)

Linda Smith (author of *Mrs. Biddlebox* and *Moon Fell Down*)

Eileen Hehl (author of numerous YA and adult romance novels)

Karen Stickler Dean (author of YA series, *Maggie Adams*)

1

My grandmother's voice was hushed, the lines of her face accentuated by soft lamplight, as she began to talk. In the quiet of night, I could almost pretend the three of us—Nona, Dominic, and I—were sitting around a campfire telling ghost stories. Instead, we were inside Dominic's loft apartment and Nona wasn't telling us tales.

The truth was far more scary than fiction.

The antique silver box she'd given me lay heavy in my lap. It was cool to the touch, with tarnished edges and raised half-moon and star designs embossed into the lid. "Pandora's Box," I'd teased when Nona had first showed it to me.

And I was right.

The contents themselves weren't dangerous. In fact, when I'd lifted the lid to look inside, I'd felt let down. I'm not sure what I expected—maybe jewels or rare coins. That would have been more exciting than a faded photograph, an old Bible, and a tiny silver charm in the shape of a cat.

"Before I explain about the box," Nona said in a shaky voice. "You should know more about my great-great-grandmother."

"Don't tire yourself." The concerned look Dominic gave my grandmother irritated me. He wasn't even related to her—a handyman/apprentice who looked about my age, but didn't attend school. All I knew was that Nona invited him to live at her farm because he possessed unusual talents. Secrets had drawn them close, and I couldn't help but feel left out.

"I appreciate your concern," Nona told Dominic with a fond smile. "But resting just wastes valuable time. The only thing that can cure me is the herbal potion my great-great-grandmother Agnes created for an aunt who suffered from the same hereditary illness I now have. It's important you understand about Agnes. She had the family mark of a seer, like Sabine."

I reached up to touch the black stripe in my blond hair. Before Nona's hair turned silver, she'd had one, too. She told me it signified amazing psychic abilities. But when I was little, I'd been ashamed of it. Kids called me a freak and said I didn't wash my hair. Once I'd taken scissors and cut out the dark streak. It grew back, but I never grew used to being different. Even now, after my gift had helped to save a friend's life, I yearned to be normal.

My grandmother was talking again, and I leaned forward in my chair so I didn't miss a word. "Agnes lived over a hundred years ago in a small town where people were expected to behave in a certain way," she explained. "Women raised children and were good wives. They dressed, acted, and even thought alike."

"My mother would fit in there," I said bitterly.

"That's probably true." Nona cracked a wry smile. "But it was a terrible place for someone with a gift."

"Like us."

My grandmother nodded. "Agnes was widowed young and had to raise her four daughters on her own. She created herbal remedies for everything from upset stomachs to bad breath. She also gave advice—telling things that always came true. She could predict the future for others, but not herself. So when she spurned the advances of the married mayor, she had no idea his anger would result in malicious rumors. Suspicious townsfolk turned away from her, whispers of witchcraft spread."

I frowned. "That's so unfair."

"When has life been fair to those born different?" Nona shook her head sadly, then continued. "When a neighbor woman became ill and died for no obvious reason, the mayor accused Agnes of poisoning her with a headache potion. That night Agnes' eldest daughter, who also had the gift, warned her mother she was going to be arrested for murder. Her only choices were to stay and risk a death sentence, or run away."

"What did she do?" I whispered, gnawing on a fingernail.

"She was brave, not stupid. A neighbor offered to care for her daughters while Agnes fled to distant cousins who had settled in the West. Her plan was to send for her daughters when it was safe. Unfortunately, that never happened."

I held my breath, imagining this heartbreaking scene. Four little girls hugging their mother, tears falling as they said good-bye, not knowing it would be their last time together. Or maybe they did know, which would make it worse.

Glancing over at Dominic, I could tell he was moved by the story, too. Was he thinking of the mother he'd lost too soon?

Nona paused for a moment, a glazed look coming over her face. I knew that look now and what it meant. I held my breath, struggling to stay quiet while she found her way back into memories. Seconds later, Nona's eyes sharpened and I let out my deep breath.

"As I was saying," Nona went on with a determined lift of her chin, "Agnes went out West. No one knows where for sure. But a year passed with no word from her—until a package was delivered to her daughters. It came with the sad news that Agnes had died and she wanted her daughters to have the box."

"This one?" I lifted the silver box.

"Exactly." Nona nodded. "Inside were four charms and a note saying the charms would lead to the hidden location of her remedy book. But the girls never got a chance to search. The friend couldn't care for them anymore and they were adopted into separate families. Before they split up, each girl took a charm as a keepsake."

I picked up the silver cat that was no bigger than my thumbnail. "Your great-grandmother chose this one?"

"Yes," Nona answered as she stared at the photo. "Florence was the eldest, so she kept the box for her most precious belongings: this charm, the family Bible, and the last photo taken of her sisters and mother. That's Florence in the middle."

She pointed to a serious-looking girl of about eight. Her hair was pulled back in a braid, and she had the same strong, straight nose as Nona. Her mother, Agnes, didn't look any older than I was; yet she'd been a wife, mother, and widow. She sat in a stiff-backed chair with her four daughters circled around her.

"You can tell Agnes loved her daughters," I said wistfully, thinking of my own mother who didn't like me much. "Did the sisters ever get back together?"

"No," Nona answered sadly. "Not in this world anyway."

I set the photograph back in the box, and lifted up the silver cat. "What did the other three charms look like?"

"I don't know. There's no record of that."

"Or of what happened to the sisters," Dominic added grimly.

"So you don't have any idea where the remedy book is?" I asked.

"No. And it's my only hope." My grandmother's gaze was haunted as she reached out to grasp my hand. "That's why I'm asking you and Dominic to find it for me."

2

*I never want to go through another day like this
again*, I thought as I crawled into bed after midnight. All the drama with my friend Danielle—
finding her bleeding to death and rushing her to
the hospital, then coming home to Nona's horrible
news. I still couldn't believe my grandmother was
losing her memories and could slip into a coma

within six months. Danielle would recover . . . but I wasn't so sure about Nona. And that terrified me.

Emptiness echoed in the soft rustle of my sheets and the eerie quiet of my room. Darkness had never been my friend. It breathed with living, moving shadows that whispered to me. So I kept a night-light lit. I had dozens of nightlights arranged in a glassed case; a collection I'd started when I was five and had been scared by my first ghost. He was harmless—a one-armed soldier who was lost be-tween worlds. Since then, there had been many other-world visitors. They didn't scare me anymore because Nona had explained the difference between ghosts, spirits, and angels. And I'd gotten close to my spirit guide, Opal.

Still, even though I was sixteen, I always slept with a nightlight.

Hoping to find help from the other side in my dreams, I chose a cat-shaped nightlight. I plugged it in and whispered a fervent prayer for Nona to get well.

Then I closed my eyes and dreamed.

*   *   *

I was one with a rain-scented breeze, soaring with a sense of freedom. I expected my dreams to carry me over a hundred years into the past, but I found myself drifting in a different direction, as if someone called my name, beckoning me to follow.

The first thing I was aware of was laughter— soft, sweet, and feminine. I saw the girl as if I was looking down from a cloud. Her hair fell in waves of caramel-brown, rippling as she twirled on an outdoor pavilion. There were others there, too: girls in tight sweaters, rolled-up socks and full mid-length skirts and guys in buttoned-shirts and stiff-looking slacks. But the brown-haired girl shone bright, leaving others in shadows. Her every move radiated like the sun. She laughed and twirled and teased. The guys begged for her attention, while the girls glared and gossiped from the sidelines. The wooden floor was her stage; she was The Star.

Then the scene changed.

Someone new arrived, parting through the girl's sea of admirers. With a single look, the tall dark-blond stranger captured her attention, curling his hand in hers as they stole the dance floor.

Lightning flashed daggers against a dark sky.

Rain began to fall on the pavilion.

And they danced.

*   *   *

I jerked up in my bed, my head spinning to an unfamiliar melody. I was drenched in sweat, and my nightgown clung to me as if I'd been caught in a storm. Blinking, I looked at my illuminated bedside clock and was surprised that only twenty minutes had passed since I'd fallen asleep.

My heart pounded like I'd been running, and I breathed deeply to calm myself.

What just happened? I thought in confusion. I'd wanted a vision of my ancestors and the remedy book. Instead, I'd been shown something very different. I didn't know who the dancing girl was, but I sensed she wasn't related to me and had no connection to the missing charms.

So why had she invaded my dreams?

I clenched my pillow. It wasn't fair! I should have control over my own mind. Did I need to concentrate harder? Perform some kind of ceremony with candles and incense? Recite a chant?

Nona would know what to do, but I resisted the urge to rush to her for help. She was counting on me now and I had to be strong for her. Besides, I could imagine what she'd advise—"Listen carefully to your dream messages because they could lead to important discoveries."

But I'd dreamed the wrong dream. I needed a vision of Agnes or her daughters—not a flirtatious dancing girl.

Stay out of my head, I thought to the girl. *I don't care who you are or what you want. I don't have time to deal with you.*

Then I tried again to connect with my ancestors. Breathing deeply, in and out, over and again until my anger faded to fatigue, weariness settled over me, and my eyes closed. . . .

A storm stirred a wicked brew of danger. I was swept along like a speck of dust, blowing wild in a dangerous wind. Dark clouds boiled and thunder rumbled. Excitement soared as I sensed a shift of time and place. Gray shrouds parted and down below on a rocky outcropping I saw a familiar figure.

The caramel-haired girl.

Not her again! Anger clouded my vision. This wasn't supposed to happen. I fought to open my eyes, to retreat from this mental cage. But wind whipped me closer, trapping me in my own dream.

Unwillingly, I watched. The girl wasn't alone. The dark-blond stranger stood beside her, his arms outstretched, imploring. Something had gone wrong, terribly wrong between them. She glared and shouted at him. Emotions swirled in reds and purples, a tornado of rage. I couldn't hear her words, but felt overwhelming anger and pain.

The world shuddered, shifted, and the scene shattered into confusing images. I glimpsed a rocky cliff, a steep drop to rocks and broken trees. A long-dead tree, split into pieces, spiked to a point like an offering to the sky.

The girl was falling, flying over the cliff's edge. Her scream, shrill and sharp, tumbled through empty air.

And then silence.

3

My alarm blared for the third time before I reached to shut it off.

"Quiet already," I grumbled, waking to a sense of dread. It took a moment for my head to clear and to vaguely remember my unsettling dreams. A girl in fifties clothes . . . dancing and flirting . . . a scream. Something horrible had happened. What? Images flitted in my mind, then slipped away. Trying to understand made my head throb. So I stopped trying. A weird dream didn't matter anyway. Only Nona mattered.

I was glad it was Saturday and there was no school. But I had a nagging feeling that something else major was happening today. Dread grew when I glanced at my wall calendar. A black slash crossed today's date. I groaned.

This evening I had to face my worst nightmare. *My mother was coming.*

I'd been avoiding her calls, making excuses not to talk to her for months. I mean, what was the point? We'd only get into another argument because I wasn't perfect like my nine-year-old twin sisters. Everything seemed so easy for Ashley and Amy. They were musically talented and attended a private performing arts school. They were tall and willowy, with Dad's satin-black hair and Mom's violet-blue eyes; a combo that was gaining them fame as models. Since they were identical, most people thought they were alike, but I knew better. Ashley was outspoken and as ambitious as our mother, while Amy was studious and eager to please.

I'd given up trying to please my mother years ago. She rejoiced in my twin sisters' talents, but my spooky abilities scared her. You'd think she'd be use to supernatural stuff after growing up with Nona, but instead it had a reverse affect. Mom lived in the land of denial and blamed me for being different. Dad accused her of overreacting. He didn't believe in anything outside the legal facts in his law library, and thought I was as normal as my little sisters. So he often took my side. But that ended when he became a partner in his law firm, and started working eighty-hour weeks. He wasn't around to defend me after I'd foretold the death of a popular football player. When even close friends turned against me and I'd been kicked out of school, Mom sent me to live with her mother. I loved being with Nona, but my mother's betrayal hurt.

I would never forgive her.

Burying my head under my pillow, I was tempted to hide in bed. I needed a long rest after all the drama yesterday. Things got out of control with Danielle and I'd risked exposing my psychic ability. Still, I was glad I'd helped save her life. I just hoped no one figured out how I'd known where to find her.

Finding the cure for Nona's illness would be much harder. Everyone involved was long dead.

Sure I saw ghosts, but they usually appeared when they wanted something from me—not the other way around. I didn't know how to contact a particular ghost. Entities on the other side didn't exactly carry cell phones. And contacting my ancestors through dreams had failed. So now what?

Since when did you forget about me? a sassy voice asked in my head.

"Opal? Are you there?" I whispered. I never physically saw my spirit guide the way I did ghosts and angels, but rather sensed her presence. I knew her proud smile and the critical arch of her dark brows well. For someone who'd been dead for hundreds of years, she could be really bossy, but she could also be a trusted friend.

Of course I'm here, she said in her usual impatient manner. *Otherwise, you would be conversing with yourself.*

I lifted the pillow off my head, keeping my eyes closed since it was easier to see Opal that way. "Can you help Nona?" I asked.

My duty is to guide you along your chosen path.

"Then tell me where the remedy book is so I can help Nona."

That is beyond my knowledge.

"Why?" I demanded.

Because I simply do not know.

"But you have to! My ancestors must be on your side somewhere, can't you ask them where the book was hidden?"

Sabine, you try my patience by failing to realize our worlds are vastly different. What matters to you is often of little consequence here. Your life is your own to live, my humble role is one of guidance.

"Then guide me to the book!"

The path to what you seek begins in your soul. Search out wisdom from those with like minds. Mistakes are inevitable and great sorrow can be a stern teacher.

"What do you mean 'great sorrow?'" I sat up straight in bed, clutching covers to my chest. "I'm not going to lose Nona. I won't let it happen."

Disease is only one way to be trapped in an earthly body and a lost soul waits to be set free. Do not withdraw when assistance is sought.

"Would you stop talking in circles and just tell me what to do?"

Do as your grandmother asks.

"I don't understand."

But you will. . . .

She broke the connection, and I opened my eyes to an empty room.

Determination pulsed through me. Nona had asked me to find the remedy book, and that's exactly what I would do. Also, I'd make Nona's life easier by taking over the housework and cooking. I could even help her home computer dating business, Soul Mate Matches, by answering phones and organizing her files so efficiently she'd never lose her computer password or important papers again.

Confidently, I sailed into Nona's office.

My grandmother sat at her desk, absorbed in the computer screen, jotting down notes with one hand while snacking on a pumpkin muffin with the other. She looked so vibrant, with shining gray eyes and rosy color in her cheeks; it was hard to believe she was ill.

"Good morning, Sabine." She tapped her keyboard, bringing up photographs of dozens of smiling women. She clicked on more keys until only a woman with reddish brown hair and a round freckled face was on the screen.

"How are you feeling?" I asked cautiously.

"Never better. I think I've found a match for Kenny Campbell. Beatrix Frayne is over thirty, loves animals, and volunteers at a Boys and Girls Club. If their astral charts are compatible, I'll arrange a meeting." She gestured to a plate of muffins. "Help yourself. They're still warm."

"Thanks," I said, reaching for one. Then I glanced around Nona's office. "How can you find anything with so many piles, folders, and boxes scattered all over?"

"It is a mess," she admitted with a chuckle. "But I have my own system."

"A little organizing couldn't hurt. Let me help."

"That's not necessary."

"But I want to," I said, picking up two thick piles of papers.

"No! Don't mix those up!" Nona flew from her chair and snatched the papers. "It took hours to compile these files of over-fifty men with musical talent. And the other pile is recently divorced Taurus women."

"Then I'll help by typing these." I turned to a box filled with Post-it notes. "You'll be able to find all the information in one place."

"Well . . . I guess that couldn't hurt."

It didn't hurt me, but Nona winced when I dumped the box on the floor and began organizing. I tried, really I did, but how was I supposed to know "Hairy Fish and Bell Frog" meant a new client named Harold Trout would be a good match for Annabelle Hopper? Just when Nona stopped me from shredding a list of new client numbers, the doorbell rang.

I rushed to answer it.

"Hey, Sabine, are you ready?" my friend Penny-Love greeted, looking like a freckled angel in jeans and boots. Her full name was Penelope Lovell, but her nickname, like her white T-shirt, was a good fit.

"Ready?" I stared at her blankly. "For what?"

"Duh." She ran her polished ruby-red nails through her copper curls. "Sabine, did you fall off the planet or something? You promised to go shopping, you know, to buy decorations for Fall Fling Dance. The Booster Club is counting on us to have everything by next Saturday."

"I forgot." I gave a rueful smile. "Things have been hectic lately."

"So I heard. I couldn't believe when Jill told Kaitlyn who told Amber who told me that you were there when Danielle was found half-dead on the football field. What happened? Why didn't you call me?"

"Sorry. Everything was crazy—rushing to the hospital and then staying until Danielle's family showed up and I found out she was going to be okay. I didn't get home till late," I said evasively. Penny-Love was great fun, but she was also a great gossip. I had to be careful what I revealed to her. If she knew a psychic vision had led me to Danielle, the news would be all over school in a flash.

To change the subject, I pointed to the driveway. "Where'd you get the car?"

"My oldest brother. He needed Dad's car to impress a girlfriend, so he offered me his rusty reject. It's not much, but it runs fine."

I looked dubiously at the rust-brown dented Mustang on our gravel driveway. One tire was half the size of the others, making the car lopsided.

"It's great you got wheels," I told her. "But you'll have to go without me."

"Why?" she demanded.

"Because Nona needs me to—"

"Nonsense," my grandmother interrupted, coming up behind me. "I don't need anything. You go out and have fun."

"I can't leave you." I shook my head. "Not until you're better."

"Nona looks better than ever to me," Penny-Love put in as she greeted my grandmother with a hug. Both romantics at heart; they'd become quick friends. "So how's the love biz?"

"Blooming like a garden! I signed up three new clients this week."

"Getting paid for matchmaking is like the best job in the world," Penny-Love said. "If you ever need an assistant, give me a call."

"It's a deal." My grandmother smiled.

"You don't need an assistant, you have me. And I'm not going to leave you alone." I folded my arms across my chest. "I want to help."

"You can help best by not helping," Nona insisted. "I know you mean well, Sabine, but I'll get more accomplished alone."

"And we have important things to shop for today," Penny-Love added firmly.

Cornered by both of them, how could I argue?

So for the next few hours, I put worries aside and shopped.

There wasn't a mall in Sheridan Valley, a medium-sized blend of suburbs and rural farms, so we drove into Sacramento. It wasn't a long drive, about forty minutes by freeway. Penny-Love had funds from the Booster Club and a mile-long list of things to buy: crepe paper, paper plates, plastic silverware, colored paper, paint, glitter, and more. When we finished, Penny-Love talked me into hitting the clothing stores and trying out extreme fashions. I tried on a wild purple plastic mini dress and she slipped into a silver sequin gown with a slit down to her belly button. We paraded around the store, receiving weird looks from other customers and suspicious looks from the clerks. Bursting into laughter, we changed back into our T-shirts and jeans, then hit the food court.

After serious contemplation, I chose Chinese and Penny-Love bought the largest cheeseburger I'd ever seen. Amazingly, she ate the whole thing—plus a jumbo platter of French fries.

Then we went into a jewelry boutique and I found a pair of funky piano-shaped earrings perfect for my sister Ashley. My twin sisters' birthday party was in two weeks, and Amy had begged me to come in her last email. Since it was going to be held at an amusement park, where I could easily avoid my mother, I'd agreed to go.

I wanted to show my sisters how much I missed them with special gifts, so I convinced Penny-Love to stop at a used bookstore. Amy collected vintage series books like Nancy Drew. I checked her list of most sought-after titles—and struck pay dirt with a shiny green book titled, *The Haunted Fountain*. When I found an autograph from the author, I knew this was a great find—and for only eight dollars!

When we returned home, I felt better than I had in days.

Until I saw the midnight-black Lexus parked in the driveway.

4

Penny-Love heard my low gasp and turned to me in concern. "What is it, Sabine? You just went totally white."

"I'm okay." I swallowed hard.

"You don't sound okay, but whatever." She glanced over at the Lexus. "Wicked car. Whose is it?"

"My mother's." I resisted the urge to run away. "She wasn't due for two hours."

"Maybe she hurried because she missed you."

I snorted. "That will be the day. She doesn't want anything to do with me."

"I don't believe it. Parents can't resist messing with their kids' lives like a bad habit. It's all, you should do this or why aren't you doing that, but we always make up and hug afterwards. It's normal to clash with your mother."

"Nothing's normal with us. It's complicated—and hard to talk about."

"You *never* talk about your family," she accused.

"There's not much to tell. My mother hates me, so I'm living here now." I took a deep breath, then stepped out of the car. "I'd better go inside."

"Will you be okay?" she asked, twirling a red curl around her finger.

"Sure." I forced a weak grin. "My mother already kicked me out of the house. What else can she do?"

I was about to find out.

Mom looked her usual perfectionist self, wearing a tailored gray suit, matching heels and an uptight smile. She started off with fake polite talk, asking about school and friends. Not that she cared. I mean, she wouldn't even look directly into my face, as if she was afraid of what she might see—or more likely— what I might see. And she kept glancing around, as if expecting a ghost to suddenly pop out.

When she turned to Nona and asked for a private moment with me, my pulse jumped. It took all my willpower not to grab Nona and beg her to stay with me.

Instead, I lifted my chin defiantly as I faced my mother. "Okay we're alone, so spit it out. What do you want?"

"Sabine, there's no reason to use that tone with me," she said. "I'm your mother and no matter what you may think, I do love you."

"Yeah. It shows."

"Are you still angry with me?"

"Of course not."

"Sending you away was harder on me than you."

"Oh, really?" I arched my brows skeptically.

"Of course. But I'm relieved it's all worked out for the best. You're doing well in school and have new friends. Your sisters tell me you even have a boyfriend. What's his name?"

I hesitated, unwilling to share something so personal, but not comfortable with a direct lie. "Josh DeMarco."

"DeMarco? Is he Italian?"

"I don't know," I said icily. "Or care."

"I was simply asking a question. I'm sure he's a charming boy, and I'd love to meet him when I have more time. It's obvious you're thriving with your grandmother. You always preferred her anyway. Instead of being angry because I arranged for you to stay here, you should thank me."

"Thank you," I said in a voice dripping with sarcasm. "Is there anything else?"

"Well. . . ." She glanced down at her clenched hands. "There is something I need to discuss with you. I came here so we could talk away from the twins."

"Why? Are they okay?" Alarm leaped in me. "Amy hasn't had a bad asthma attack, has she?"

"No, nothing like that. But I'm concerned about Ashley's friend, Leanna."

I'd never heard the name. "What does that have to do with me?"

"Leanna is the younger sister of that boy from your last school." She pursed her lips. "The one who died."

Guilt and pain slammed into me, but I masked my emotions with a shrug. "So?" I folded my arms across my chest. "That still has nothing to do with me."

"But it does," my mother insisted. "Leanna will be at your sisters' birthday party. It could be awkward and remind everyone of that unpleasant time."

"I'll stay out of her way."

"I'm afraid that won't be enough."

My stomach clenched. "What do you mean?"

"If you love your sisters, make sure they have a happy birthday."

"How?" I asked icily.

She met my gaze squarely. "Don't come to their party."

5

I couldn't talk about Mom's request, not even to Nona. My heart ached too much, and talking about it wouldn't solve anything. Besides, Mom was right. Although I'd never met Leanna, she would recognize me as the "freak" who predicted her brother's death. I'd warned him not to drive on prom night, but he'd just laughed about it with his pals. Only no one was laughing when he died in a fiery crash. Instead they pointed fingers of blame at me, as if knowing made me guilty.

And I loved my sisters too much to ruin their birthday.

How am I going to tell them I can't go to their party? I thought, blinking back tears. *Say I have a date? Fake a contagious illness? Or just blow them off like I don't care? Lying is horrible, I hate it! But what other choice do I have? My lie will be like a secret birthday gift to my sisters, so they can keep believing Mom is perfect and I'm the screw up.*

It was so hard, wanting to do the right thing yet not sure what would hurt my sisters more. Finally, I made what seemed like the hardest decision of my life. Before I chickened out, I went to my computer, logged online, then typed a short email:

Amy and Ashley,
Something came up and I can't make your party. Sorry. Happy birthday. Love Sabine.

Then I hit "Send."

After that, I kept too busy for thinking, feeling, hurting. Since Nona wouldn't let me back in her office, I tackled housework. Then I stayed up past midnight embroidering a pillowcase with delicate pink roses. The next morning, after washing and folding four loads of laundry, I shrugged into my jacket and went outside to gather eggs.

A sliver of sunshine broke through the gray sky, then disappeared behind puffy white clouds. The ground was damp with dew and fallen leaves crinkled under my boots. I tightened my jacket, rubbing my chilled hands together.

The basket was nearly full with brown speckled eggs when I heard a motor rumble and saw Dominic by the barn starting up his truck. His secondhand Ford had some dents, but was dependable. Dominic had proven himself dependable too. He'd helped me out of a few tough situations, and I was learning to trust him. Still we weren't exactly friends, more like reluctant allies.

Penny-Love practically drooled over Dominic, flirting outrageously when he was around. He was good-looking, I guess, if you went for the surly, mysterious type. But I didn't. I'd already found the perfect guy. Josh was tall, athletic, and so considerate he volunteered regularly at hospitals. How could I not fall for someone who made sick kids laugh by pulling stuffed rabbits out of bedpans?

Josh embraced humanity, while Dominic avoided people, preferring to work outdoors with animals.

"Hey, wait!" I called to Dominic, setting my basket on the porch as I rushed over to his open truck window. "We need to talk about Nona."

"When I get back," Dominic said briskly.

"How long will that be?"

"Don't know." He had an irritating habit of speaking in short sentences—when he bothered to speak at all.

"You're planning on being gone awhile or you wouldn't have packed." I pointed to the worn brown suitcase on his passenger seat. "Where are you going?"

"Astoria."

"Oregon? But that's over five hundred miles away." I narrowed my gaze. "Does this have something to do with Nona's remedy book?"

He shrugged. "Depends."

"Depends on what?"

"If I find it."

"We're supposed to work together. You can't just leave without telling me anything. And who will take care of the livestock while you're gone?"

"It's been arranged."

His calm tone infuriated me. "Shouldn't you tell Nona that you're leaving?"

"Did already."

"But you didn't bother to fill me in on whatever lead you're following. That's not how partners work. If you found out something important, I demand to know what it is." I grabbed the edge of the car window. "You're not going anywhere till I have some answers."

I expected him to yell at me to get out of his way. But instead losing his temper, he broke into a smile. "You think you're strong enough to stop my truck?"

"Probably not."

He chuckled. "But you'd try anyway?"

"Sometimes trying is all you can do."

"I know," he said with a nod. "You're good at it."

Our eyes met and we weren't talking about the truck anymore. Energy sizzled between us, making me hot and uncomfortable, like wearing a wool jacket on a sunny day. I didn't understand these feelings, nor did I want to. Dominic and I only had one thing in common: my grandmother.

"Okay, partner, here's the situation," he said briskly, shutting off the truck's engine so the yard was suddenly quiet. Even the chickens ceased cackling. "I've been making calls and checking records for Florence Jane Walker Tuttle."

"Nona's grandmother?" I asked eagerly. "What did you find?"

"I tracked down this guy, Alex Tuttle, who has old pictures of a distant aunt named Agnes."

"Our Agnes?"

"Don't know. But I plan to find out."

"So you're driving all the way up the Oregon coast? Couldn't you just ask on the phone?"

"Not if I want to look through family albums."

"Albums?"

"Very old family albums."

"Wow. I'd love to see them."

"So come with me." He held out his hand invitingly, his fingertips brushing against my arm.

I jumped back, my skin tingling where he'd touched. "You can't be serious."

"Why not? We are *partners*." He spoke the word in a soft, teasing way and he studied me with a look that made me uneasy.

"But—I can't just drive off with you."

"Why not? Afraid?"

"Of course not!" I faked a laugh. "Not even."

"Then get in the truck."

"I can't! I have school tomorrow."

"Skip it."

"I wish I could—for a lot of reasons." I shifted uneasily on the driveway. "But I have responsibilities, like the school newspaper, homework, and my friends."

"Your wannabe magician boyfriend?" he asked with a sneer.

"Leave Josh out of this. And shouldn't you have some kind of school, too?"

"Not me." He grinned wickedly. "Besides, I got to move on this fast. Tuttle may have more than old pictures."

"Like what?"

"Welll. . . ." Dominic drew out the word deliberately. "He mentioned a trunk of old books."

"And?" I prompted.

"One of them could be the remedy book."

6

I appreciated Dominic's dedication to helping Nona, but I resented being left out and wanted to be the one to find the remedy book.

Remembering Dominic studying me, as if he could see through my clothes, added to my sour mood. What was it with him anyway? Why had he invited me to go with him? He usually shunned the human race, so his sudden offer was confusing.

Maybe he felt sorry for me because I'd failed to find results on my own. Well, I'd show him! While he drove to another state after clues, I'd find out more right here.

And I knew just where to start. Agnes's Bible. Taking out the thick, brittle book, I fluttered through age-worn pages and made a list of births, marriages, and deaths going back almost two hundred years. My family tree branched across paper with mostly unfamiliar names. So many unknown, forgotten relatives with tragedies and triumphs recorded in brief passages.

By the next morning, I had twelve pages of information in my notebook—and I was eager to show it to Dominic. Only there was no word from him yet. I jumped whenever the phone rang and kept listening for the sound of a truck. Nona didn't seem concerned, and assured me we'd hear from him when he had news. Her voice rang with hope, and I was relieved she'd showed no signs of illness. Instead, she was like a super woman, already in her office making calls before I'd even started breakfast.

There was nothing for me to do, except go to school—which I *so* did *not* want to do. The news about Danielle nearly bleeding to death on the football field would be Gossip Topic #1. And if anyone found out about my part in that drama, I'd become Topic #2.

Penny-Love met me on the way, and I was relieved she didn't even mention Danielle. Old news already, I thought hopefully. Instead Penny-Love went on and on about the Fall Fling Dance: what she was wearing, the guy she planned to ask, and elaborate decorating plans.

Relieved to slip into my normal routine, I only half-listened. It was like there were two Sabine's, one who could act like a dance was as important as world peace, and another who heard voices and had psychic visions. Guess it was no accident my sign was Gemini. I never talked about weird stuff at school. Mostly, I did a lot of listening. Especially with Penny-Love. It's funny how people liked you when you let them talk. After being run out of my last school, it was a relief to be accepted and even popular.

Penny-Love was the Queen Bee of Sheridan High. A self-proclaimed diva, she knew everything about everyone, sometimes even before they knew. She filled me in the latest three D's: dating, dumping, and dissing. I nodded at appropriate pauses and tried to pay attention. But my mind kept wandering back to the cozy yellow house on Lilac Lane. How was Nona doing alone? Had her up-beat attitude been real or an act? Why was I wasting my time at school when she might need me? I had a strong feeling I should have stayed home.

At my locker I found out why.

"Well if it isn't Sabine," a voice spoke low and menacing. "I was wondering when you'd show up."

An icy chill swept over me as I faced Evan Marshall. Tall, with broad shoulders and narrowed dark eyes, he stood in front of my locker. His aura sparked with crimson and a green as dark as night-forest. His scowl was evidence he still blamed me for ruining his friendship with Josh. But it was his own deceit that backfired on him.

"Move aside," I ordered. "You're blocking my locker."

"Are you always this rude in the morning?" he drawled, bending slightly to look into my eyes.

I wanted to fire back with some witty comment, but what was the use? I didn't have the energy to educate jerks. So I just glared and repeated, "Move."

"Sure, sure—after we have a little talk."

"I have nothing to say to you."

"Really?" His sarcastic smile made me shiver. "Not even about poor, crazy Danielle?"

"Have some respect. She *was* your girlfriend."

"I know, and I felt bad when I heard she was in the hospital. So I went to visit her yesterday."

"You did?" I asked, startled. "How did your *new* girlfriend feel about that?"

"Shelby said it was cool that I cared about an old friend, and that I'm the sweetest, nicest guy she's ever met."

"She needs to get out more. Now would you please move aside so I can get to my locker."

"Not until I thank you for helping Danielle," he said with barbed sarcasm.

"Me?" I shook my head. "I don't know what you mean. I didn't do anything."

"Oh don't be modest. I know what happened Friday night." He leaned in closer and ominously lowered his voice. "The nurses wouldn't let me talk with Danielle, but I had a long conversation with her father. And he told me some amazing things. About you."

I gulped and glanced down at the cement ground.

"How did you know Danielle was in trouble?" Evan demanded.

"A lucky guess."

"You guessed she was bleeding to death on the football field at night?"

It did sound kind of far-fetched when he put it that way. I twisted the end of my braid. "The bell is going to ring and I need my Lit book. I don't have time to waste arguing with you."

"Who's arguing? I'm just asking some questions."

"And blocking my locker."

"Oh, am I?" His eyes glittered dangerously. "I am *soooo* sorry. I didn't mean to inconvenience you and waste your valuable time. Thanks to you, I have tons of free time. You got me kicked off the football team and turned Josh against me. I owe you so much and I totally believe in payback."

"Move out of my way!"

"Not until you answer one question."

"Get lost!"

"What's your secret?" he persisted. "I knew there was something strange about you from the start. Josh wouldn't listen to me when I warned him you were trouble. It's like you've cast a spell on him. He's blind to you, but I'm not. You're hiding something. I don't know what it is . . . but I'm going to find out."

Then he made a sweeping gesture toward my locker, stepped aside, and walked away.

7

I was still reeling from Evan's threat when Josh showed up.

"Were you just talking to Evan?" he asked, frowning as he peered down the hall where Evan had turned around the corner.

"Uh . . . yeah." My heart was still pounding, and I felt a wild sense of paranoia. Like I wasn't safe anywhere, not at school or home.

"Was he bothering you?"

"Uh, not really." I grabbed some books and slammed the locker shut.

"Then what did he want?"

I glanced at my Lit book. "He asked about our homework assignment."

"Really?" Tension eased into a wistful smile. "He told me he was getting serious about homework, but I had my doubts. If he improves his grades, he'll be back on the team."

I bit my lip. "He needs to improve more than his grades."

"Don't be so hard on him. Sure, he made some mistakes but he's a cool guy once you get to know him."

"I know more than enough."

"Evan told me he felt bad for those things he said about you."

"You're talking to him again?" My heart lurched. "After everything he did?"

"He lives next door and our parents are friends. I can't just ignore him and I don't want to. Everyone needs a second chance. I feel bad how things turned out."

"It wasn't your fault."

"Yeah, I know. But it's hard to stay mad. I keep thinking of all the good times we had, and even the bad times when my brother was sick. Evan stuck by him until the end. I've got to stick by him, too, I owe him that much."

"You owe him nothing."

"Maybe." He shrugged, but his tone wasn't convincing. He lifted his head as the warning bell rang. "We better hurry to class."

I nodded, uneasy about Evan's influence over Josh, especially after Evan's threat to find out my "secret." If he did, he wouldn't hesitate to destroy me.

As Josh and I walked, he described his weekend trip to attend a cousin's wedding. I debated over telling him the truth. It would be a huge relief to be honest, but I was afraid he wouldn't believe me. If I explained about my spirit guide, ghostly dreams, and the prophetic vision that led to a boy's death, he'd think I was delusional.

Before we entered our first period Lit class, Josh ripped out a piece of paper from a notebook. With lightning quick fingers, he folded it, smaller and smaller, rounding the corners, sharpening the end to a point, until I recognized the shape.

"For you, Sabine," he said, holding out a paper heart.

Words swelled up my throat and I hugged the paper to my chest. He put his arms around me, drawing me close. His touch was gentle and his light brown hair smelled fresh with a scent of lime shampoo. Not caring if anyone was watching, I lifted my chin and met his lips in a gentle kiss.

And I vowed to never do anything to risk losing him. At school I would be totally normal. No more "weird" stuff.

Still, I had to figure out a way to help Nona. I decided to get advice from a trusted friend who already knew my secrets. So I told Josh that I couldn't eat lunch with him because I had some last minute work to do on the school paper.

As expected, I found the editor of the school, Manny Devries, in front of a computer terminal. Manny's black hair was twisted into cornrows, and he sported a new pierced arrow-shaped eyebrow ring. He wore black zippered jeans and leather sandals. It could be snowing and he'd still wear sandals, not even harsh weather could dampen his style.

When he saw me, he flashed a pearly grin. "What's up, Beany?"

I hated that nickname, but let it pass because I needed his help. Manny was a born snoop, and darned good at it. He'd discovered what happened at my last school and agreed to keep my secret. In return I helped with predictions for his "Mystic Manny" newspaper column. Whenever I heard people rave about his amazing talent for predicting the future, I smiled.

Now I glanced furtively around the classroom, checking to make sure we were alone. The only other person present was Mr. Blankenship, but he was busy grading papers. "I need some advice," I whispered to Manny.

"Lay it on me, Beany." He rolled a chair next to him and gestured for me to sit down. "Tell Uncle Manny everything."

"Don't patronize me. This is serious."

"Don't I look serious?"

"Not with that cocky grin."

He pressed his lips into a stern line. "Is this better?"

"Now you look like a demented psycho." I lightly punched his shoulder. "Stop kidding around.

Nona is in trouble and needs me to find an old book."

"So ask Thorn. She's the finder."

I paused to consider this. When Manny first introduced me to his Goth friend, Thorn, she'd wowed me with an amazing skill for finding things. But I was put off by her brash attitude, multiple body piercings, and metal-spiked collar. If I wanted to stay cool with my other friends, hanging out with a Goth chick was a bad move. She wasn't any more eager to be seen with me. But she'd been quick to help when I needed her, and I discovered a kindred soul underneath the Morticia makeup. Like me, she'd been born with a psychic ability. Psychometry, she called it. Only she was cool with her skills, while I was still dealing.

"This is beyond Thorn's talents," I told Manny. "What I'm searching for was lost a long time ago."

He arched his pierced brow. "How long?"

"Like a hundred years, give or take a decade. To track it down, I need to find out about my ancestors. But I don't know where to look."

"No problem." He spun around to his computer. "I know tons of genealogy sites. Tell me the names and I'll find the information."

I almost fell over with relief. "It's that easy?"

"Did you ever doubt me?"

"I'll tell you when you deliver the answers."

"Oh, I will. But it'll cost you," he added with a wicked chuckle.

Tilting my head, I asked cautiously, "What?"

"I'm writing another ten years in the future spotlight for the paper, and I could use your all-knowing insight. My victim—er, subject—is a freshman named Jayvon Bonner. Peek into your crystal ball for me and I'll check the computer for you."

"I can't promise results, but I'll try."

"Fair enough." He scratched his chin. "So whom should I look up?"

*   *   *

In fifth period, during a particularly boring assignment, my mind drifted and just like that I knew Jayvon Bonner's future. He'd move to Colorado and train as a figure skater, only an ankle injury would end that career. Then he'd move to New York and work off-Broadway on set design. His artistic talent would eventually lead him to a successful career as an illustrator of children's books.

When I met Manny in our sixth-period class, he was delighted when I handed him the paper. His black eyes shone with discovery and I knew he'd found out something, too. When I asked, he put his fingers to his lips. "Too many people around," he whispered. "Wait till after class."

So I went to work on my job as proofreader for the school newspaper. It was an easy job that gave me an "in" to school happenings with zero personal risk. Usually, I enjoyed my work. But the article I'd been assigned to edit, describing a chess tournament, was totally brain numbing. I was relieved when the bell rang and kids swarmed out to freedom.

I strode over to Manny's desk. "Out with it!"

He flashed a cocky grin. "First tell me how brilliant I am."

"Whatever." I rolled my eyes. "You're brilliant."

"That didn't sound sincere."

"Your brilliance is so enormous, the only thing bigger is your inflated ego. Is that sincere enough?"

He laughed. "Beany, you kill me."

"Don't tempt me. So did you find out what happened to Agnes's daughters?"

"No. That search came up empty." He tapped the eraser end of a pencil on his desk. "But by checking town records, I found info on the woman who took care of Agnes's daughters after she left. Martha Poindexter Kabkee, born 1863, died 1943."

"How does that help?" I asked, discouraged.

"If she kept in touch with the sisters after they were adopted, there could be a document trail. Letters, postcards, diaries. Martha's descendants may know something."

"But how do we find them?"

"Already started." Manny held up a computer printout and I leaned in closer.

"There's only one name listed here."

"Martha had one son, who had two children but one died young. So that leaves her granddaughter who by coincidence lives in California. Not very far away either, a retirement resort in Pine Peaks."

"Where's that?"

"Up in the Sierras, not far from Lake Tahoe."

I nodded, feeling hopeful. "So did you call her?"

"Affirmative. But she's on a cruise till Friday. I'll give you the number and you can call her then."

"That won't work," a voice interrupted and I turned around to find a petite raven-haired girl dressed in black leather. "No one will tell you anything important over the phone."

"Thorn!" I gave a start. "How long have you been standing there?"

"Long enough to know you're looking for some old lady." Thorn's purple-black lips curved into a smile. "But you're going about it all wrong."

"What do you think we should do?" I retorted.

"Why call when you can go there in person?" Her smile widened. "It just happens I have an aunt who lives in Pine Peaks and she's been begging me to visit. So I'll drive you."

8

The next few days flashed by with a flood of activity. Packing, getting permission to miss school Friday, collecting homework in advance, and calming a panicked Penny-Love who was counting on my help with the Fall Fling Dance.

"I'll be back by Saturday afternoon," I promised her as we walked to school Wednesday morning. "Don't worry."

"Worrying is what I do best," she said lightly.

"And you do it so well. But seriously, no way am I missing the dance. I've already got the perfect dress—and the perfect date to go with it."

After school, I checked my list of everything I had to do. I hated leaving Nona, but at least Dominic was back and I knew he'd keep an eye on her. Unfortunately, his trip had been a total failure. He'd returned in a dark, discouraged mood. It turned out Mr. Tuttle drank too much and lied for sport. There were no journals, no distant Aunt Agnes, only a filthy living room littered with empty bottles.

I felt bad for Dominic, but hopeful for myself because when I'd consulted with Opal she'd hinted that I'd find answers in Pine Peaks. I imagined this scene where I handed Nona the remedy book. She'd burst into grateful tears and throw her arms around me. Dominic would be so overcome by admiration and congratulate me on my success. "I didn't think you could do it, but you proved me wrong. You're amazing," he'd say. Then he'd hold my hand, look into my eyes and pull me close. . . . WAIT! What was I thinking anyway?

That night the dancing girl returned to my dreams.

Surrounded by male admirers, she laughed and flirted, her full skirt whirling as she took turns dancing with each young man. When the handsome stranger appeared, the dream changed from light to dark, and they faced each other on the ragged cliff. He reached for her, but she pulled back and shouted at him. I couldn't make out her words, but I felt sadness so deep, as if hearts all around the world were breaking.

A wind whipped up, a storm brewing with thunder and black clouds.

Don't go near the cliff, I tried to warn the girl. But everything sped up as if I was being swept along in a tornado. Someone was running, flying through rocky ground, and over the cliff. Falling, down toward the jagged trees below. Only it wasn't the girl this time—it was a man. I couldn't see his face, but a startling fear jolted me awake.

And I had an awful feeling that the falling man was someone I already knew—or someone I would know soon.

9

The next morning Nona remembered her breakfast date with her friend Violet, but forgot to change her clothes. If I hadn't ran in front of her car to stop her from leaving, she would have shown up at the diner in a silky blue nightgown and pink fuzzy slippers. It would have been funny if it wasn't so tragic.

I was ready to cancel everything and stay home to care for my grandmother. But Nona wouldn't hear of it. I begged her to let me miss school, but she got that stubborn look and I knew it was hopeless. Besides, we both knew this trip offered hope at curing her illness.

After school, Thorn drove up in a yellow jeep and I climbed into the passenger seat. Once on the road, Thorn popped in a CD and cranked up the volume. I didn't recognize the band, but the lead singer was brilliant and he was very sad about something. She mouthed along to her music like I wasn't there.

Just great, I thought in dismay. *There's nothing more fun than being ignored on a long road trip.*

Shifting in my seat belt, I stared out the window at crowded developments with houses so close together you could walk from roof to roof. The San Jose neighborhood my parents lived in was like that; massive houses with tiny yards, landscaped to appear as natural as the forests and fields they'd replaced. I'd had a back bedroom with a small patio where I'd sit for hours, doing crafts, drawing, or dreaming. Sometimes Amy would sit beside me and read quietly. Then Ashley would join in, get us talking, until we were all laughing.

I miss them, I thought, the world outside the window blurring. *But they probably hate me now, thinking I don't care enough to go to their party.*

Swallowing a bitter taste, I shut off my thoughts. The scenery changed as we gained elevation; housing developments gave way to rolling green hills with spindly elms and maples brilliant in golds and reds. Dying leaves flamed with glorious beauty. I imagined myself a falling leaf, letting go, flying free, soaring away on a strong breeze.

Then the jeep hit a pothole and I smacked my elbow against the door.

"Ouch!" I rubbed my elbow. I glanced over at Thorn to see if she even cared, but she kept on mouthing along to her ear-shattering music.

How do I get her to open up? I wondered. I'd hoped to get to know her better on this trip. Thorn was the first person my age I'd met who had a psychic ability. And her aura, unlike her dark clothing, glowed with lavender and yellow. She intrigued me like a wrapped package, the contents unknown. And they'd remain unknown if Thorn wouldn't even talk to me. I needed to shake things up a bit.

So I reached out and shut off her CD player.

"What do you think you're doing?" Thorn demanded. With exaggerated black eye makeup and painted black fingernails like sharp claws, she reminded me of an angry raccoon. "I was listening to that!"

"So was everyone within a hundred mile radius."

"Great music should be shared. The louder, the better."

"Tell that to my aching eardrums."

"You could have asked me to turn it down."

"I tried, but you didn't hear me." Then I added, "Besides, I want to talk."

"Well, I don't."

"Why not?"

"I'm just uneasy about—" She jerked to a stop at a red light.

"Uneasy about what?"

"Nothing important. Besides, what would we talk about?"

"Whatever you want."

"My friends and I usually talk about poetry, graveyards, and vampirism. What do *your* friends talk about? Planning what to wear to the Fall Fling Dance?"

"Well . . . more than that." I didn't add that I was on the decoration committee. Afraid she'd turn back on her loud music, I added quickly, "But that doesn't mean we don't have stuff in common. Like being psychic."

"So I can find things." She shrugged. "It's nothing special."

"Manny thinks it is. He calls you a 'finder.'"

"He's full of crap, but a good guy."

"I know what you mean." I nodded. "He's outrageous, yet so honest about it you can't help but like him."

"It's crazy what he gets away with. The more outrageous he is, the more girls want him. Every week he's got a new girlfriend."

"Sometimes two," I joked.

She laughed, giving me a quick glimpse of a silver stud in her pierced tongue. "Since you want to talk, I got a question for you."

"Fire away," I told her.

"What's the deal with your grandmother? I heard you tell Manny she was sick, only she looked fine to me."

I frowned. "It's hard to talk about."

"Talk or I'm turning up the CD full blast."

"Well. . . ." I paused, finally deciding I owed her an explanation. "Okay, but swear you won't repeat this to anyone."

"Done. My promise is sacred." She crisscrossed her black-painted fingernail across her chest. "So what's wrong with your grandmother?"

"Yesterday she got up early to feed the livestock. Then an hour later, she went to feed them again and asked me if I'd fed them. She tried to cover up by joking, but I knew she'd totally forgotten. And this morning she almost went out to breakfast wearing her night clothes."

"So what? Older people forget stuff a lot."

"It's more than that." I took a deep breath and then described Nona's illness. When I finished, I was surprised to see compassion in Thorn's gaze.

Neither of us spoke again for miles. Silence hailed around us, a harsh third companion. I was tempted to turn the radio back on and blast away the quiet.

Instead, I turned to Thorn. "You asked a question, now it's my turn."

"Whatever," she said with a shrug I guess meant yes.

"Is Thorn your real name?"

"It's real enough. Better than what my parents chose."

"Which is?" I prompted.

"Not something I'm going to tell you or anyone else."

"So tell me about your family."

"I'm nothing like them. My parents are okay, I guess, although they don't know what to do with me. And putting up with three sisters and two brothers is insane, so I don't spend much time at home."

"What about a boyfriend? Do you have one?"

"Not at the moment," She pursed her purple lips stubbornly. "What about you?"

"Yeah," I nodded proudly. "Josh DeMarco, you've probably seen him around."

"Dark hair, looks hot in tight jeans?"

"That's him," I grinned. "So can I ask you one more question?"

"Depends on the question."

"Why a banana-yellow jeep? I figured you'd drive something wicked to go with your Goth look, like a black hearse."

"A dead mobile would be cool." She glanced up at her rearview mirror, then turned back to me. "But this is Mom's jeep. She insisted I take something with a four-wheel drive since a storm is predicted. She worries too much."

"At least she cares."

"Yeah. For an uptight suburbanite, Mom is okay. I don't have to pretend with her anyway. I just wish that other. . . ."

"Other what?" I asked.

"Nothing. Just family issues."

"Well...your Mom sounds nice. You're lucky." Sadness washed over me, and suddenly I didn't feel like talking. I turned back to the window and Thorn turned her music back on.

It was dark when we reached our turn off. I noticed Thorn tensing up, twisting her hair and chewing her lower lip. I was tempted to ask what was wrong, but figured she'd just blow me off.

Closing my eyes, I tried to read Thorn's energy. But there was nothing. Like tuning into a radio station and only getting static.

"Why are we stopping?" I asked when Thorn pulled into a gas station. "You still have half a tank of gas."

"I won't be long," she said briskly, grabbing her duffel bag. "Wait here."

Then she hurried off into the gas station.

And I waited.

Five minutes, then ten, passed. I know because I was staring at my watch, counting each second. Worry jabbed me like sharp needles. What if she'd gone to the restroom because she was sick? She hadn't looked good when she'd left. Even underneath ghostly-white face makeup, I could tell she was pale. And she seemed really uneasy. Was she afraid of something?

Another five minutes passed and I'd had enough.

Flinging open the car door, I headed for the public restroom. The door wasn't locked, and when I peered inside I saw a young girl with a sweet face and short dark blond hair, wearing a striped blue skirt and virgin white sneakers that reminded me of a prissy school uniform. She didn't look up and continued washing her hands in the sink. I moved past her and checked out the three bathroom stalls. The doors hinged open and no one was inside.

Thorn had vanished.

10

Stunned, I turned to the young blond girl. "Where's my friend?" I asked.

"Huh?" She turned off the faucet and gave me an amused look. "What friend?"

"The black-haired girl. She came in but she never came out!"

"Oh . . . her." She wiped her hands on a paper towel and tossed it in the trash. "She's gone."

"Where'd she go?" I asked anxiously, all the while staring at this girl and getting the oddest vibe. Her aura was familiar . . . and that wasn't all.

When I gasped, she doubled over laughing. Then I knew for sure. But I still didn't quite believe what I was seeing.

"Thorn, is that really you?"

"Well, duh." Even with a fresh scrubbed face and different clothes, I recognized her sarcastic grimace. "Don't make a big deal about it."

"But you're so different."

"So what?" She shrugged.

"Without any makeup, you look about twelve."

"I do not. And I'm seventeen—older than you."

"What happened to your black hair?"

She gestured to her duffel bag. "It's in there."

"A wig?" I said in amazement as we climbed back in the yellow jeep. "You've been wearing a wig all this time? And your real hair is blond?"

"Dark blond. Boring like everyone else in my family."

"Why not just dye your hair?"

"Tried that, but had an allergic reaction. So I mix it up with black wigs. Short, long, spiked—whatever fits my mood."

"Why switch back to blond now?"

"You'll find out," she said ominously, then started up the engine and snapped on her CD. Conversation over.

As we drove, I kept sneaking glances at Thorn. The illuminated car panel cast a soft yellow glow, making her appear angelic, as if she wore a mask.

It was dark and drizzly when we slowed to turn into a rural gravel driveway. A single yellow bulb glowed over the front door of a ranch-styled house. As we drew near, rubber on gravel rumbled like a warning, lights flashed on from inside. And the door burst open.

"Brace yourself," Thorn murmured, and I wondered if she was talking to me or herself. She killed the engine, took a deep breath, and stepped out of the jeep. I hesitated only a moment before following.

"You're here!" a middle-aged woman exclaimed, rushing forward with her arms outstretched. She wore a pink robe, slippers, and had her brown hair pulled back in a waist-long ponytail. "Charles," she shouted back toward the house. "Come on out and greet your niece!"

A thin scarecrow of a man appeared in the doorway, and he buttoned up a coat as he hurried forward. While the woman embraced Thorn, he came up beside them and affectionately patted Thorn's shoulder.

I stood back, not sure about my role in this happy reunion. Then the woman glanced up and noticed me. She broke away from Thorn and suddenly I was wrapped in a soft, warm hug.

"You must be Sabine," she gushed.

I nodded shyly.

"Why you're as pretty as a sunflower." She stepped back to look at me. "But much too thin. How long has it been since you girls ate? Well, no matter, come on inside, I have dinner warmed up for you. I hope you like spareribs, broccoli, and mashed potatoes. And I baked a carrot cake for dessert."

My stomach growled appreciatively. "Thanks Mrs. . . . uh. . . ."

"Matthews. I should have introduced myself right away, only I assumed you'd know all about us." She patted Thorn affectionately on the arm. "But then our baby-girl Beth has never been very talkative."

I opened my mouth to say, "Who?" Only Thorn moved quickly to my side and jabbed me with her elbow. The look she gave me translated to "Shut up!"

But I just covered my mouth so I wouldn't burst out laughing.

Rough, prickly Thorn was "baby-girl Beth."

*   *   *

"It's bad enough being named after a character from Little Women." Thorn scowled a few hours later, as she hung a red skirt in the closet of the guestroom we were sharing. "My sisters are Jo, Meg, and Amy."

"I have a sister named Amy, too."

She shrugged, like having something in common with me was just another annoyance. "And my brothers are named after the book too. Lawrence and Al—for Alcott. But I get the name of the sister who dies. How pathetic."

"It could be worse," I said, squeezing toothpaste onto my brush from the doorway of the adjoining bathroom.

After I was finished, I plugged in a candle-shaped nightlight and climbed under a hand-stitched patchwork quilt. Crystal bowls with pine needles and roses gave the room a sweet, fresh scent—a homey touch that added to the warm hospitality we'd received. Mrs. Matthews was an excellent cook and a gracious host. Her husband hadn't said much at first, but then he opened up with funny stories about "Beth." When she was little she found a "lost kitty" which turned out to be a baby skunk and another time she'd made a secret fort in her room by smashing a hole in her closet.

Thorn snapped off the bedside lamp between our twin beds. "What's with the nightlight?" she asked curiously.

"Nothing." I pretended a sudden interest in fluffing my pillow.

"Are you afraid of the dark?"

"Why would you ask such a thing?" I said sharply. "If the light bothers you, I'll turn it off."

"No, it doesn't bother me. I kind of like it."

I said nothing, but felt relieved.

"Although there is something bothering me," Thorn added more seriously. "You found out stuff today about me that I don't want to get around."

"Don't worry. I won't tell."

"You'd better not."

I couldn't resist teasing, "Not even Manny?"

"Especially not him!" She rolled her eyes. "I'd never hear the end of it."

"Your secrets are safe with me," I assured, pulling the blankets up around my shoulders. "But why pretend with your aunt and uncle? They seem really nice."

"It's because they are nice that I can't disappoint them. They never had any kids and they kind of half-adopted me. They think I'm a sweet, innocent little girl and they'd freak if they saw me in black makeup. I couldn't hurt them."

"Watch out Thorn or you might develop a heart," I said lightly.

"You watch out or I'll smash your face."

"Anything you say . . . Beth."

"Don't call me that!" she growled.

I ducked as she threw a pillow at me.

11

I awoke to the delicious smell of bacon and sound of sizzling eggs. Thorn's bed was empty, and when I glanced at my watch, I was startled to see I'd slept past nine-thirty. Quickly, I slipped on my clothes and raced downstairs.

Before I could say "Good morning," Mrs. Matthews had me sitting at the dining table and was serving me a plateful of hot blueberry waffles.

She insisted I call her "Aunt Deb" and kept urging me to eat more.

Mr. Matthews sipped coffee and told more stories about "Baby-Girl Beth." He chuckled over the time two-year-old Beth, who wasn't quite potty trained, had an accident in a neighbor's brand new hot tub. Thorn turned as red as the strawberry preserves spread on her toast. I would have felt sorry for her if I hadn't been laughing so hard.

Afterwards, Thorn and I offered to wash and dry dishes. When we were through, her uncle gave us directions for Peaceful Pines Senior Resort. We were finally on our way to learning about my ancestors. I was excited, but nervous, too.

"We should have called first," I said as I buckled my seat belt.

"And spoil our element of surprise?" Thorn started up the jeep. "Not a chance. We'll learn more if we just show up."

"As long as we aren't the ones surprised," I added with a glance up at dark clouds blowing across a gray sky. The temperature had dropped and the air smelled of rain. I didn't need psychic skills to know a storm was brewing.

Pine Peaks was a small mountain town with only a few blocks of quaint businesses along Pine Street. So it was a shock to get stuck in a traffic jam. A posted sign announced a population of only 835, but it looked like that number had tripled. Cars were squeezed in every available space and the only motel had a no-vacancy sign.

"What's the slow-up?" Thorn slapped the dashboard. "Don't they know small towns are supposed to be peaceful?"

"Nothing small or peaceful about Pine Peaks today," I said, looking around curiously. "Wonder what's going on."

After waiting for three light changes of a street light, we found out. A large banner was stretched across the arched entry into a park announcing: "Pine Peaks' Ninth Annual Chloe Celebration."

"Chloe?" I read, puzzled. "Who's that?"

"Like I know or care." Thorn swore as the traffic slowed to a complete stop. "My aunt warned me the roads would be busy, but I didn't believe her. And now we're stuck in some groupie fest. Where did all these people come from?"

"That van is from Sacramento." I pointed to a white van with a radio station's logo painted on the side. "And look over there—isn't that Heidi from Channel 3? The newscaster with the perky—"

"Check out the license plate in front of us!" Thorn interrupted with a low whistle. "Florida."

"—smile," I finished. Then I pointed to a red car. "There's a Texas license plate."

"And that parked truck is from Arizona," Thorn added. "This Chloe chick must be really hot."

"A famous singer or actress," I guessed, studying a crowd of people milling on the sidewalks, all wearing identical yellow T-shirts.

"Being famous doesn't give her the right to screw up the traffic," Thorn grumbled. "That baby stroller is moving faster than we are. I've had enough! I'm going to find out what's going on."

"How?" I asked.

"Watch me."

She rolled down her window and called out to the group of yellow shirts. "Hey! Can someone answer a question?"

The yellow shirts turned to Thorn, then spoke among themselves. After a few minutes, a pear-shaped woman wearing retro black-and-white saddle shoes stepped forward. She was probably over thirty, but seemed younger with her curly black ponytail bobbing as she moved.

"Hello!" she greeted with a smile that revealed blue-tinted braces. "Can I help you?"

"Yeah." Thorn pointed to the T-shirt. "What's everyone celebrating?"

"We gather here every October to see Chloe," she said as if that explained everything.

"Chloe who?"

"Don't tell me you haven't heard of her!" The woman's voice rose with astonishment. "She's famous!"

"Not to me." Thorn shook her dark-blond head. "Is she around here somewhere?"

"She's everywhere and nowhere." The woman spread her arms out wide. "If the weather cooperates we'll see her soon."

"Oh," Thorn said with an arch of an eyebrow that looked bare without its usual pierced stud. "Will she cancel her performance if it rains?"

"On the contrary. She only appears in the rain. Lightning storms are even better."

"Huh?" Thorn gave me a sideways look and I shrugged. If this woman was an example of Chloe fans, we wanted far away fast. I hoped the street light would hurry up and change.

"I'm the president of Chloe's fan club and helped organize this event. Our main anniversary celebration is Saturday night, but if there's a storm tonight we'll gather at the pavilion. Come join us," she invited. "If we're lucky, Chloe may make an appearance."

"You go to all this trouble for someone who might not even show up?" Thorn asked incredulously. "Chloe sounds like one rude diva."

"She has a long distance to travel."

"That's no excuse. She can just hop into her private plane to meet her fans."

"If only it were that easy," the woman said with a good natured sigh. "But we can't expect her just to show up whenever we want."

"Why not?" Thorn demanded.

"Because Chloe has been dead for fifty years."

12

"Why would anyone celebrate a ghost?" Thorn asked as we pulled into Peaceful Pines Resort. "It's worse than those people who still think Elvis is alive."

"You mean he isn't?"

She gave me a shocked look, then lightly smacked my shoulder when she realized I was teasing.

"It's cool people still care about Chloe so many years later," I added as I unfastened my seat belt.

"There's nothing cool about this. It's all a freak show to get tourist business. Come to our town and see a ghost. Ha! I bet the whole thing is a big fake."

"Why couldn't it be real? It makes sense that Chloe shows up when it rains. With electricity in the air, the connection to the other side is more open."

"Of course you know everything about ghosts," she said with an edge of sarcasm.

"Not even—but I've seen a few. Haven't you?"

Thorn shook her head firmly. "No."

"Never?"

"Nope. And I don't want to."

"Why not?" I asked, a little disappointed we didn't have this in common. "Most people want to see someone they loved one last time."

"Well, I'm not most people. I keep telling you, finding is just a game for me. I don't have any other special abilities. I don't want some ghost to pop in while I'm taking a shower. When people are dead, they should stay that way." She was protesting too much, and I sensed she wasn't telling me the whole truth. Was she afraid of ghosts? I wondered.

Before I could ask, we reached the office and entered a door marked "Manager." A jingling bell announced us, and a petite woman carrying a longhaired Chihuahua in the crook of her arm stepped forward. Her swept-up hair was a silvery blond and her wrinkled neck contrasted her unnaturally smooth face.

"Good afternoon, I'm Helen Fontaine. What can I do for you?" she asked in a voice more shrill than her yapping dog.

"We're here to see Eleanor Baskers," Thorn said politely.

"Oh, you are?" Helen's dark eyes pooled with curiosity. "Ellie never mentioned having granddaughters, only grandsons."

"We're not related to her," I explained.

"I didn't think so, not with that blond hair." She turned from me, furrowing her brows as she studied Thorn. "But your face is familiar . . . do I know you?"

"No." Thorn shook her head. "I'm not from around here."

"Are you sure? That upturned nose and the way your mouth curves on one side . . . I know!" She snapped her fingers. "You're one of Deborah's nieces. Which of the Little Women are you? Amy, Meg, or Beth?"

"Uh . . . Beth." Thorn's cheeks blushed first-degree-burn red.

"Oh, the one that dies . . . in the book, that is." She laughed. "Your aunt and I go way back. I was her Sunday School teacher and—"

"We can't stay long," I interrupted, coming to Thorn's rescue. "How do we get to Mrs. Baskers's cottage?"

"It's Number 261. Only she's not there. She's away on a Caribbean cruise."

Thorn frowned. "But she's supposed to be back today."

"Her plane was delayed by a bad storm in Florida," Helen answered as she stroked her dog's smooth fur. "Ellie called a few hours ago to say she wouldn't be back until tomorrow."

"Tomorrow!" I cried, my hopes sinking fast.

"Sorry, girls. Come back then and I'm sure she'll be happy to talk with you." A phone rang and the Chihuahua started yapping again. Shushing the dog, Helen waved good-bye, then whirled off to answer the phone.

"Now what?" I sighed deeply as Thorn and I left the office, the jingling bell over the door sounding so cheerful I wanted to smash it.

Thorn shrugged. "We come back tomorrow."

"But that means staying another night. Will your aunt and uncle mind?"

"They'll hire a band and throw a parade in our honor. They love having us."

"They've been great, only I hate waiting around here accomplishing nothing." I paused on the brick path, looking around at towering pines and an overcast sky that seemed to close in on me. I wondered how Nona was doing. I should be there with her, not so far away.

"So we'll do something," Thorn suggested. "Wanna check out the local shops?"

I cupped my ear, not sure I'd heard right. "Is shopping allowed in the Goth Code of Conduct?"

"Page 50, Paragraph 2, says the only rule for Goths is we don't have rules." She shrugged with attitude. "Besides, I find great stuff at thrift stores. Once I found a roll of barbed wire for only a dollar that I twisted into a wicked belt."

"I'll pass on the barbed wire accessories."

"So buy something touristy. Like one of those lame Chloe shirts."

"Only if you get one, too."

"No way."

"But a yellow shirt would go great with your jeep," I teased.

"My mom's jeep, not mine." She reached out to swat me, only I dodged to the side then hurried ahead down a rock path.

The path led to a beautifully manicured park with wicker benches and flower gardens. The damp air carried a whiff of freshly mowed grass. Beyond shady trees, I glimpsed cozy white stucco cottages. I wondered which one belonged to Eleanor.

I heard Thorn call my name and turned back. I caught up with her by a ranch style clubhouse. As we passed a large picture window, laughter echoed from inside the building. Curiously, I peeked through the glass and saw several elderly people crowded in front of a large screen TV. Another group gathered around a card table, each protectively studying their cards. And off alone in a quiet corner, a frail red-haired woman reclined in a blue cushioned chair. She wore a familiar yellow T-shirt with black letters that read: "We Love You Chloe."

Another groupie! Why is Chloe so popular? I puzzled. *Is it is because of her life or her death? What magic did she have that brings flocks of people to this tiny town fifty years after her death?*

A strong curiosity came over me. I had to know more.

"Where are you going?" Thorn demanded.

"Inside." I walked around to the door and stepped into the clubhouse.

No one barred my way to ask what I was doing here. The card players ignored me and the TV watchers laughed at an old *I Love Lucy* episode. So I crossed the room toward the lone woman.

Up close her hair was more pink than red, reminding me of cotton candy. She wasn't holding a book as I'd expected, but an electronic game. She hunched over the game, her fingers clicked keys rapidly, accompanied by musical sounds of beeps, crashes, and booms.

She hadn't noticed me, so I tapped her shoulder. "Excuse me. . . ."

Startled, the woman jumped. Her hands slipped from her game and an explosion blasted. The tiny screen went dark.

She whirled accusingly. "You killed my wizard!"

"I-I didn't mean to," I stammered.

"I would have beat my highest level if you hadn't interrupted."

"I was just trying to get your attention."

"Well you certainly did that. I didn't even get a chance to save my score." With a groan, she tossed her game aside on an end table.

"I'm sorry." I didn't know what else to say, and held out my hands in apology.

"What's done is done." She shrugged, then surprised me with a smile that showed off pearly dentures. "I'll simply try again later. So what do you want?"

"Nothing much . . . I mean, I just wanted to ask about your. . . ." I flushed with embarrassment. "Your shirt."

"This silly thing?" She plucked at a fold in her T-shirt. "I got it at Tansy's Trinkets for $13.95. But you can find them just about everywhere in Pine Peaks."

"A lot of people were wearing them when we drove through town."

"What do you expect?" she asked with a shrug. "It's October."

"But why all the interest in Chloe? I never heard of her before today. All I know is that she died fifty years ago."

"Fifty-four years to be exact." The elderly woman's faded blue eyes gazed into space, as if she were seeing the past. "The whole tragedy could have been avoided if Chloe had listened to me."

"You actually knew her?"

"Better than anyone. She was my dearest friend. We were together so much, people mixed us up, calling me Chloe and her Cathy. My father nicknamed us the 'Stormy C's' because we could get really wild."

It was hard to imagine this frail cotton-candy-haired woman as "wild." But I nodded, encouraging her to continue talking. Call it perverse, but this whole ghost celebration intrigued me.

"We did everything together," she explained. "We made up silly lyrics to our favorite songs, practiced dance steps, and double-dated. Of course, her parents were so strict they didn't allow her to go out much, so she'd sneak out the basement window. Since our birthdays were two days apart, our families combined our parties. But it's not Chloe's birthday they celebrate now." A bitter shadow crossed her wrinkled face. "It's her death day."

"How'd she die?"

"It's too terrible to talk about. They called it an accident, but I knew better." Cathy's thin lips pursed and her eyes narrowed with fury. "It was *his* fault."

"Who?"

"I won't speak ill of someone no longer around to defend himself." She shook her head. "But if it weren't for him, Chloe wouldn't have gone out that night. She would have married Theodore and still be alive. She was engaged to Theodore and he adored her. It was a secret, but of course I knew all about it."

"Theodore must have been heartbroken when she died," I said softly.

"She broke Teddy's heart long before that. She was my friend and I loved her, but I didn't approve of how she treated Teddy. He deserved someone better."

Like you? I wondered. "What happened to him?"

"He had a long distinguished career in the Navy, becoming an admiral. When he retired, he moved here into the cottage next to mine. He never married and won't talk about Chloe. I'm the only one who ever visits him. All the fuss over Chloe, yet the Chloe Museum doesn't even mention their engagement."

"Chloe has her own museum?" I asked, astonished.

"Seems a bit silly, doesn't it? That's what a lot of us thought when it opened up fourteen years ago, but now it's the hottest tourist spot in Pine Peaks. It's the old brick building beside the barbershop. Fellow by the name of Kasper runs it."

"Is that a bad pun? Casper the Ghost running a museum for a ghost?"

"Kasper with a K." She smiled approvingly. "I'm surprised someone so young remembers old cartoons."

"They're on the Cartoon Channel. I don't watch anymore . . . but I used to." With my sisters, I remembered with a sharp pang. Sure, they could be annoying, but we had good times too. Like if my parents were gone on a weekend, I'd make them pancakes in animal shapes and we'd watch cartoons.

"Be sure to visit the museum while you're in town," Cathy added. "Kasper will tell you plenty about Chloe. It won't all be true, but it'll be entertaining."

"I'd rather hear more about Chloe from you."

"I've said enough already. But you can find out plenty in this week's *Piney Press*. Here." She handed me a newspaper from the end table. Then she wished me luck and turned her game back on.

When I stepped outside, I didn't see Thorn. So I walked to the parking lot and found her waiting by the jeep.

"You took long enough," she said.

"Sorry. But I found out some interesting stuff."

"About what?"

"Chloe," I answered simply. "I talked to her best friend."

"A ghost has a best friend?"

"They knew each other when they were young. She gave me this newspaper and said there's an article about Chloe."

"Cool. Let me see."

I handed Thorn the paper and we unfolded it together. A bold headline on the front page jumped at me: "Record Breaking Attendance for Chloe Celebration." Below this caption was a black-and-white snapshot of a beautiful girl with wavy dark hair. She wore a mid-length skirt and a snug sweater that showed off her ample curves. Her sweet, sultry smile was inviting, yet harbored secrets.

I must have gasped, because Thorn asked what was wrong. But all I could do was stare at the paper. I now knew how Chloe had died.

She'd fallen to her death over a cliff.

And I'd seen it happen . . . in a dream.

13

"Are you okay?" Thorn asked as we neared Pine Peaks and had to slow for traffic. "You haven't said a word for miles."

"Just tired."

"It's more than that. This has something to do with Chloe. What's the big obsession?"

"Nothing."

"I don't buy it. You're acting weirder than usual. Did you have one of your visions or see a ghost?"

"So you *do* believe in ghosts?" I countered.

"Well, duh." Thorn rolled her eyes. "I figure everything is possible. But I don't go around talking to ghosts like you do."

"I do not. Mostly I try to shut them out. Although it's hard to ignore my spirit guide Opal. She loves to nag me."

"Spirits, ghosts . . .What's the difference?"

"A lot." I shifted in my seat to face her, relieved to switch the topic. "Spirits are people who made it safely to the other side. They can come back to visit and sometimes appear in dreams. But ghosts are confused and usually don't realize they are dead. So they're stuck here."

Stuck here. Those words echoed in my mind and a dark sense of foreboding sent a shiver through me. My hands clenched together so tightly my knuckles turned white. Thoughts and images added up to a clear revelation. My coming to Pine Peaks was no accident. Eleanor Baskers probably had zero information about the missing charms. I'd been summoned here through dreams, lured by a ghost. This trip wasn't about Nona anymore.

Chloe was in charge.

I hated being manipulated. But I had a feeling Chloe would keep haunting my dreams until she got what she wanted—whatever that was.

"I need to see the museum," I told Thorn.

"You're buying into all the Chloe hype? Are you serious or showing the first signs of insanity?"

"Both." I forced a calm smile despite a strong urge to run from a growing sense of danger.

"You are definitely nuts," Thorn said with a shrug. "But it could be a kick, and we have time to kill. So let's go."

Finding the museum was easy. Finding a parking space was nearly impossible. But when Thorn went after something, nothing stopped her. After weaving through side streets, she zipped into a spot as another car pulled out.

A large redwood plaque arched over the doorway: "Chloe Museum." Entering the brick building was like walking into a tomb. The chilly air smelled of ages past. Shivering, I tightened my coat around my shoulders.

We stepped into the parlor lit by cone-shaped lamps on wooden end tables. There was a scent of lemon and fifties music played softly in the background. The décor was totally retro; an overstuffed olive-green couch and matching loveseat circled an oval glass-topped coffee table and thick shag carpet that muffled our footsteps.

"This reminds me of my grandmother's house," Thorn said, poking a puffy green couch pillow. "I bet there's a kitchen with ugly checkered linoleum, too."

"Looks like we go down that hall." I pointed to a wooden sign directing us to the museum.

Following the posted arrows, we stepped through French doors into a large open room with bright overhead lights. The dampness was gone, but goose bumps rose on my arms.

"Welcome!" boomed a cheerful voice. The elderly bald man who stepped out from behind a clothing display was as round as a beach ball. The yellow T-shirt stretched across his chest had to be a size triple X. And his grin seemed even wider.

"Uh, hi," I said uneasily. "We're looking for Kasper."

"Congratulations—you found me!" he said with a twinkle in his eye. "What can I do for you pretty ladies? How about a genuine Chloe souvenir? All red-tagged items are on sale today, ten percent off. Take your pick from T-shirts, key chains, shoe laces, dolls, hats, socks, and toothbrushes."

"Toothbrushes?" Thorn arched her brows. "People actually brush their teeth with Chloe toothbrushes?"

"Why of course! In glamorous shades of pink, blue, and red. But it's the refrigerator magnets that sell best. Would you like to see our selection?"

"We'd rather hear more about Chloe," I replied, slowly turning a rack of post cards. I picked one up with a picture of Chloe at a dance. She wore a full, mid-length skirt that swirled in a breeze on an outdoor pavilion.

Just like my dream, I thought uneasily.

"Well, you've come to the right place," Kasper said. "I'm a scholar of the unexplained and have written numerous books on the paranormal topics. I know everything about our famous ghost."

Thorn tilted her head at him. "Have you actually seen her?"

"Sure. As clear as I see the two of you."

I raised my brows, tempted to point out that few people saw ghosts *that* clearly. I knew he was exaggerating, but saw no reason to spoil his fun.

"After I retired," Kasper went on, "I found Chloe so fascinating, she became my hobby."

"I've never heard of anyone having a ghost for a hobby," Thorn said.

"Well, now you have." He slapped the counter and laughed as if he'd told a hilarious joke. "This very building you're standing in is seeped in Chloe history. This was her home for all of her seventeen years and I've recreated the rooms in exact detail from old photographs."

That led to an invitation for a personal tour (waiving the usual two-dollar fee), and we went from room to room, seeing everything "Chloe." Flowered skirts, tight-knit sweaters and a closet full of shoes, including pink ballet slippers and the black–and–white saddle shoes from my dream. School yearbooks and old board games—Scrabble, Life, and Uncle Wiggley—were stacked in a corner. Clunky metal skates with a shiny key were sprawled on a fluffy white rug. And an entire wall of portraits charted Chloe's growth from infant to teenager. It was eerie to see her so vibrant, so alive.

Her friend Cathy had to be in her seventies, but Chloe never aged.

Seventeen forever.

When we finished the tour, I asked for directions to the restroom. Going downstairs, through a side hallway, I made a quick potty stop. But when I came out, I got turned around, because I found myself in a darkened hall that dead-ended at a wooden door with a fist-sized red heart painted on it.

"Sa-bine," came a breathy whisper.

"Who said that?" Now it was my own heart thumping wildly. I looked around fearfully, seeing no one, yet sensing I wasn't alone.

"Sabine."

I covered my hands over my ears, but my own name echoed like a curse inside my head. Icy darkness seeped out from the door. But I didn't back away. Instead I moved closer, compelled by forces I didn't understand. I reached for knob and—

"Get away from there!"

Jumping back, I turned to find Kasper striding over. His fleshy face was reddened and his mouth pursed tightly. He grabbed my arm. "That room is off-limits!"

"Why?"

"Because it's not safe," he blustered. "You shouldn't be here."

"Sorry, but I got lost."

"I'll show you the way back."

Shadows shifted and energy flowed behind the door, and I was oddly reluctant to leave. I pointed to the door. "What's inside?"

"Spiders and rotting wood." He drew a handkerchief from his pocket and wiped sweat off his forehead. "I keep it locked for safety reasons. The stairs are old and dangerous, and I can't afford a lawsuit if someone falls. I hardly ever go down there."

"So who painted the heart?" I asked.

"I don't know. It was there when I bought the building fourteen years ago. Probably the work of a bored kid." He seemed flustered as he nodded towards the hall were Thorn waited. "Come on. I can't leave my store unattended any longer."

Returning to bright lights and tacky souvenirs was jarring—as if we'd traveled through a time capsule from decades past. And the image of the delicate red heart stayed with me.

Had the voice calling my name been from Chloe? I wondered as I browsed through aisles of cheesy merchandise. Had she wanted me to open the door? Was something hidden inside that Chloe wanted me to find?

When I saw a biography on Chloe's life, I couldn't resist picking it up. Flipping through the pages, I skimmed the first chapter. I was pierced with a sharp sense of connection, despite our differences. She'd been outgoing, flirtatious, and aspired to become a famous actress or dancer. I was more serious with no lofty ambitions. I didn't want to stand out, I longed to fit in.

So why was Chloe reaching out to me?

While Thorn sorted through videos of black-and-white movies, I made four purchases: Chloe's biography (written by Kasper), a Chloe toothbrush (I mean, who could resist something so cheesy?), and two yellow souvenir T-shirts.

"Thanks for visiting and come back again," Kasper said, banging the cash register shut. "I'll walk you to the door."

I shook my head. "Thanks, but you better stay here to answer your phone." And sure enough, as I said the word "phone," the phone behind him rang. The startled look Kasper gave me was priceless.

Smiling, I hurried to catch up with Thorn who had already left the museum. As I glanced up at the sky, a raindrop splashed on my face. Overhead, dismal gray clouds swirled and I heard an ominous rumble of thunder. There was a light touch on my shoulder, but when I turned to look, no one was there. When I glanced down at the ground, a faint impression of a heart appeared in the cracked cement.

The icy chill tingling up my spine had nothing to do with the weather. Chloe was sending messages, not unlike when I'd had a vision of a dragonfly tattoo. I hadn't wanted to get involved then, and had tried to shut out the visions. But I'd finally surrendered to my gift—and ended up saving Danielle's life.

But Chloe is already dead, I thought, confused. *It's too late to save her.*

Curiosity swept through me with a storm of question marks. Who was the dark blond stranger? What was behind the heart door? Why did Chloe keep appearing in October rains? Why had she summoned me?

But I reminded myself that I didn't have time to chase a ghost. This whole trip was to help my grandmother. After I talked to Eleanor Baskers, I'd go home. Of course, I had the rest of the day free to do whatever I wanted . . . or maybe what Chloe wanted. The only thing I knew for sure was that if I did nothing, I'd find out nothing.

Thorn was crossing the street, and I waited for a break in traffic to join her.

"It's starting to rain!" Thorn covered her head with her hands.

I lifted my chin, soft drops falling on my face. "Perfect weather for ghost watching."

"If you say so." Thorn shrugged. "Those obsessed Chloe fans will be thrilled. Bet they'll be out in force tonight at the pavilion."

"Yeah." I gave her a solemn look. "And two more."

"Who?" Her eyes widened. "You don't mean?"

"Yes, I do. It's crazy, but I have to see Chloe." I clutched the shopping bag close to my chest. "Let's go ghost hunting tonight."

14

After dinner, Thorn played dominos with her aunt and uncle. They invited me to join them, but I wanted to call my grandmother. Despite the distractions from Chloe, I'd never stopped worrying about Nona. Only when I called her, the phone rang and rang and rang. Why wasn't she answering the phone? Was she meeting a client? Having dinner with a friend? Or lying injured on the floor?

You're just being paranoid, I told myself. *Nona is fine. Besides, Dominic is there to help if she has any problems. So stop worrying already.*

I set down the phone, then headed to the family room to join in the game of dominos. But when I peeked into the room, Thorn and her aunt and uncle were laughing so cozily, I was reluctant to intrude.

I used to play games like that with my sisters, I thought wistfully as I watched silently from the doorway. I remembered years ago when I'd taught my little sisters to play poker. Since Mom didn't approve of gambling, we played outside in our tree house. We didn't have money for betting, so we used M&M's. Whoever won a hand ate their winnings. It was impossible to keep score, but no one cared. And we laughed in the same connected way Thorn was laughing now.

I swallowed a lump in my throat and turned away.

Back in the guestroom, I closed the door behind me and sank on the bed. I didn't want to think about my messed-up family, so I picked up the book I'd bought earlier: the biography of Chloe Anne Marie Talbot.

Rain pounded lightly on the window as I slipped back in time. Seventeen years wasn't long enough to fill many pages, so the book was padded with numerous pictures and newspaper articles—a picture of four-year-old Chloe posing prettily on a pony at a county fair, one of her strutting in a bathing suit as the newly-crowned Miss Pine Cone Princess, and dozens of her in school plays. She was also involved in numerous clubs and committees, as if she was determined to make an exclamation mark on the world.

By her sophomore year, there were subtle changes in the photos—a sly arch of dark blond brows and an invitation in her sultry smile. There were always guys hanging around her, as if mesmerized.

I skimmed through the chapter on her family. Chloe was an only child of older parents who gave her everything, yet governed her life with strict rules. Mr. and Mrs. Talbot never missed a Sunday at church and were active members of their community. I was startled to find out Mr. Talbot was a lawyer, like my own father.

The next chapters gave an overview of Pine Peaks in the fifties. There were many news clippings of prominent citizens, and lots of dull details about politics. But what I wanted to know—had to know—was what happened to Chloe.

So I jumped ahead to the last chapter, titled "The Last Dance."

Every Saturday night she would iron her best skirt and go to the pavilion. Then she would fly on saddle shoes for hours, floating across wooden slats, flirting and teasing, but never giving her heart.

Then one rainy day in October, a handsome stranger known only as James drifted into town. He was different than the country beaus who clamored after Chloe. He was a sophisticated sweet talker with an air of mystery. When their eyes met, it was magical. After that, every dance belonged to James. They twirled and laughed and fell in love.

Chloe's family and friends warned her not to trust the stranger, to settle down with a young man from her many suitors, but she ignored them, following her heart. And when James asked her to go away with him, she agreed to meet him at the pavilion.

It stormed that night, and Chloe ignored warnings to stay inside. Rain fell heavily around the pavilion as Chloe waited. Time passed, hopes were dashed. No one knows for sure what happened, but her friends believe that when James didn't show up, her grief forced her into a wild dance, swaying and spinning to music only she could hear as her world stormed.

Perhaps she stumbled or simply lost her way. But

when the sun broke through clouds the next morning, her lifeless body was found not far from the pavilion, at the bottom of a cliff. Some say the fall killed her, but others know it was a broken heart.

And the mysterious stranger was never seen again.

So where did James go? I wondered as I stared through the window at the rain pounding the tree branches. Had he gotten cold feet and run away like a coward? Or had something terrible happened to him? If he'd truly loved her, how could anything keep him away? And how did my dream fit in? James had been with Chloe on the cliff. But according to the book, he'd never shown up.

Poor Chloe, I thought with a sigh. She risked everything for love. I can't imagine loving anyone so fiercely. It's not a real love anyway, more like obsession. I'd rather be with someone I admire and respect . . . like Josh.

Yet it wasn't Josh's face that flashed in my mind. Instead I saw ice-blue eyes and sandy brown hair. Hands rough enough to pound nails, yet soft as silk when caressing an animal. And a smile that could be as sad as tears.

Get a grip! I told myself. *What are you thinking?*

Jumping up, I slammed the book on Chloe.

Then I went to play dominos.

15

All that was missing was the music.

If this were a movie, haunting music would play eerily in the background as Thorn and I made our way down a dimly-lit street that bordered a graveyard. No stars or a moon, only inky darkness and a drizzling rain that kept falling as if the sky was in mourning. A perfect night to meet a ghost.

"This is totally insane," Thorn must have said a dozen times. But I noticed an excited gleam in her eyes. "I don't know why I let you talk me into this."

"You could have waited in the car."

"And miss all the fun?" She laughed, holding tight to a blue umbrella. "Still I felt awful lying to my aunt about visiting a friend. She'd freak if she knew what we were really doing."

"Technically you didn't lie." A gust of wind caught my umbrella, but I held on firmly. "We are going to visit a friend."

"Only you would consider someone dead for fifty years a friend."

"I consider you a friend, too."

"Oh, thanks," she said with a roll of her eyes.

We grew silent as we walked down the narrow country road leading to the park, where the pavilion rose tall and white against black night. We passed wild prickly rose bushes that grew in the ditch beside the graveyard. Through iron fences, pale headstones rose in eerie tribute to those loved and lost.

Beside me, Thorn tensed and I could tell she was nervous. Nona had told me never to fear a graveyard, that they're only haunted by memories of the people left behind. But I wasn't so sure. . . .

We stepped through the park's stone archway onto freshly mowed grass and moved toward the pavilion where a crowd gathered. Their dark umbrellas reminded me of black birds flocking to feast on scattered crumbs. Beyond the pavilion rose a rocky hill that jutted out then dropped off sharply into a canyon. The cliff, I realized with a shudder.

Bright artificial lights caught my attention and I saw Newscaster Heidi under a tomato-red umbrella, checking her makeup in a compact mirror. Her crew huddled under a flapping tarp, protecting their equipment. The last thing I needed was to accidentally get filmed at a ghost festival. If anyone from school saw me, it could be disastrous. So I planned to stay far away from the cameras.

"When will she appear?" I heard someone ask.

"When it's completely dark," came a reply. "Any minute we'll be told to shut off all flashlights and they'll cut the pavilion lights."

Thorn nudged me. "What's that music? It's familiar."

"It should be. We heard it over and over at the museum today," I said, not adding that I'd heard this song in a dream before I even knew Chloe's name.

"Yeah, that's it." Thorn snapped her fingers. "*Dance Away Love*. Kasper was selling the CDs for half price. What a gimmick. He comes off all jolly like a bald Santa, but he's only after a quick buck. He didn't even live here when Chloe died."

"You can't blame him for being a good businessman. Look, isn't that him now?"

"Yeah. Talking to that dark-haired woman. She's familiar. I've seen her before."

"We both have," I agreed, watching as the woman left Kasper in the crowd and made her way to the raised pavilion. "Only she was wearing a yellow Chloe shirt at the time instead of bobby socks and a poodle skirt. She's the one who told us about Chloe. The fan club president."

The woman folded her dripping umbrella as she stepped onto the covered pavilion. She held a microphone and moved with authority. As she took a commanding position, the crowd burst into enthusiastic applause.

"Welcome!" she addressed the audience. "I'm delighted to see all of you here tonight. As most of you know, I'm Monique Montes, President and Co-Founder of the Chloe Club and I'm delighted to see you all again for our Annual Chloe Celebration." She shielded her eyes from the glare of the TV camera and added, "It's almost time to turn off the lights and invite Chloe to join us."

"This is so bogus," Thorn muttered beside me.

"In a few moments, we may witness an amazing sight," Monique went on with a dramatic wave of her hands. "Some of you are here for the first time and others, like myself, have been coming every October since Chloe first appeared here nine years ago. For Chloe to show herself, conditions need to be perfect. So close your eyes and push out all thoughts of negativity."

"That means you," I whispered to Thorn.

The music grew louder, drowning out the sound of drizzling rain. Monique ordered everyone to turn off flashlights and cell phones. Her tone reminded me of a teacher giving a test as she added, "Our guest of honor is easily startled. So I implore you to keep quiet."

"No one saw Chloe last year," Reporter Heidi shouted with a silver flash of a microphone. "Can you comment on that?"

"How can anyone explain the unexplained? Although, you may remember, it didn't rain last year."

"Well it's raining now." Heidi's golden hair glowed under camera lights. "Does that mean we're in for a real-live ghost show?"

"Not without quiet and total darkness," Monique retorted.

Heidi got the message, and the camera lights flashed off. But I noticed a faint red glow and suspected they were still filming with special night cameras.

Monique stepped off the pavilion, snapping open her umbrella and melting into the audience. Someone shut off the music. Around us voices faded to silence.

"Do all these people really expect a ghost to come on schedule?" I whispered to Thorn, my umbrella lightly tapping hers as I leaned closer. Even with a jacket, damp cold chilled me.

"Looks like it," she said with a nervous glance around. "Don't you?"

"It's always unexpected when I see a ghost." *And a little scary*, I thought to myself.

"Well I don't expect to see anything. This is commercialism at it's worst," Thorn said so loudly that someone nearby shushed her. She lowered her voice only slightly as she added, "Someone dressed in a sheet will appear, convincing everyone they've seen a real ghost. Then they'll rush off to buy more souvenirs. I'll give it twenty minutes, then I'm out of here."

I didn't blame her for being skeptical because I had my doubts, too. And my fingers were so numb I could hardly feel them holding my umbrella. If anything was going to happen, I wish it would happen soon.

I got my wish.

Something in the atmosphere changed. Lights flickered on and off over the pavilion. Flash, flicker, flash . . . then total darkness. For a moment, everything was silent and eerily still. Then a mist rolled like gray clouds over the pavilion. Pinpoints of lights swirled into a foggy shape that swirled and swayed with unearthly life. And confusion rippled through the crowd.

"It's her!" someone behind me exclaimed.

"Where?" several people asked.

"On the stage!"

"But there's nothing there!"

Oh, but there is, I thought as a luminous shape hovered over the center of the pavilion. A misty girl with caramel brown hair and a mid-length full skirt.

"Chloe," I murmured.

"Do you really see her?" Thorn asked in a puzzled tone. "All I see is fog."

"It's Chloe all right."

Around me people chattered excitedly, some able to see Chloe and others not. The ghostly figure twirled, then slowed to a stop and lifted her arms towards her spellbound audience. I sensed sadness, longing . . . and anger.

"She's looking for the guy she loved," I whispered to Thorn. "James."

"And I'm looking for her, but I can't see anything."

"It takes a lot of energy for ghosts to materialize and even then only some people can see them. James is probably dead, so she won't find him. Not in this world anyway."

But even as I spoke, I felt an inner tug. A connection to Chloe that bound us together across space and time, like an invisible cord. The intensity of it scared me.

Okay, I'm here. I called out to her with my mind. *Now what? Why have you been in my dreams? What do you want from me?*

She threw out her arms and twirled—faster, faster, faster. Although I stood still, some part of me moved with her, spinning with grief and confusion. Together, we were trapped in a hopeless dance of heartache.

In my head, I heard her cries, *James . . . James . . . James.*

The crowd had quieted. Light sprinkles splattered on umbrellas while everyone stared at the pavilion—spellbound. I'm not sure what they saw, maybe no more than night mist. But there was a hush, as if everyone was holding their breath. Waiting.

Thorn leaned close to me. "What's happening?"

"She's dancing on the pavilion."

"Chloe?"

"Yeah."

"You're kidding, right? There's nothing there."

"She's like a faint mist. I can see right through her."

"Well I don't see anything at all. This is bogus."

"It's real. Maybe you don't see because you don't believe. Chloe led me here because she wants something. . . ."

"What?"

"I don't know. . . ." My head throbbed. "I can hardly think . . .I have to go to her."

"Don't be crazy."

"Too late," I said with a wry smile.

Then I handed Thorn my umbrella and took off running. Instead of going ahead to the raised stage, I veered away from the crowd. Creeping low, I stayed out of sight and circled around to the back of the pavilion.

My thoughts were clouded, as if controlled by someone else. My legs moved with a will beyond my own. At first no one noticed me. But when I climbed up on the back edge of the raised platform, startled murmurs rose through the crowd. I floated in a dream; none of this seemed real and my sole focus was Chloe.

"I'm here." I told her, not sure whether I spoke aloud or in thoughts. My body trembled. I was close enough to touch Chloe, but my fingers would only pass through air. She was as transparent as moonlight.

When I sent my energy out to her, she seemed to grow more solid. Her mouth curled up in a wistful smile and she lifted out a hand toward me.

James? I heard her somewhere inside my head.

"No, I'm Sabine. You called me. What do you want?"

James . . . James . . .

"He's not here. And you shouldn't be either."

Where are you James?

"I don't know where he is." I sucked in a cold breath. "But I think he's waiting for you."

Her eyes blazed with quick anger. *I waited and waited . . . always waiting . . . for James.*

"He's been gone for over fifty years," I said
more firmly. "He can't come back, but you can go
to him. Look for the light—"

I can't . . . have to wait . . .

"For what? A guy who lied to you?"

No, NO! Caramel hair rippled in angry waves
as she shook her head. *He didn't mean it . . . know
he loves me.*

"It was a long time ago. You're stuck here because you're confused. You have to let go so you
can find peace on the other side."

No peace for me or for the betrayer.

"What betrayer?" I gasped. "What do you
mean by that? It happened so long ago, you have
to understand that James can't come for you. You'll
be happy if you go to the light."

There is no light. Only forever darkness. Thunder
rumbled overhead, and her translucent body sizzled
as if electrified. Her face sharpened, hardening with
icy rage, and a red shape appeared on her chest—a
ruby-red heart like the one on the forbidden door.

Frightened, I backed away, but she advanced
toward me, her heart now seeping red, spilling
around her in a bloody tide.

Soon my waiting ends, she said ominously. *The
betrayer will fall . . . and you're going to help me.*

16

Before I could say anything else, the overhead lights flashed on.

Blinded by the intense brightness, I shut my eyes.

When I opened them, Chloe was gone.

The lights seemed to break the spell I'd been under, and maybe the audience, too. Everything went crazy. Chaotic voices rose excitedly as people shoved their way to the pavilion. They swarmed forward like an angry mob, shouting and pushing. I blinked, like a sleepwalker shocked awake. For a confused moment I wasn't sure what I was doing on a stage. Then memory crashed in and I panicked. Backing away, I whirled and leaped to the ground.

Then I ran.

Footsteps crunched behind me, so I ran faster. I kept replaying Chloe's last words. She was crazy if she expected me to hurt someone. No way!

Behind me, footsteps came closer. Fear choked me and I kept running. I wasn't even sure where I was heading, just far away.

A rock rolled beneath my foot and I stumbled. My arms flailed, but I managed to steady myself. There was a sound behind me. Before I could turn, someone grabbed my shoulder.

"Let go!" I struggled to break free. "Leave me a—"

"Chill Sabine, it's just me."

"Thorn?" I wiped raindrops from my eyes as I whirled to stare at my friend. "Wow, am I glad to see you."

"You're soaking wet. Here, take this." She handed me my umbrella.

"Thanks." I pressed the release and the umbrella sprang open. I'd hardly noticed the rain before, but now I shivered from the cold.

"Why didn't you wait for me?" Thorn demanded. "There's a reason why I didn't sign up for the track team. I hate running."

"Sorry . . . and thanks."

"What were you thinking anyway?"

"I don't know." Shudders rippled through me. "I can't believe I was up there—the pavilion—in front of people. But it was like I was walking in a dream. I must have been insane."

"It was weird, but it's over now. You can relax."

"Relax? Doubtful." I gave a shaky laugh, looking around at the rocky ground and realizing with a shock where I was. In my haste to get away, I'd run uphill and now stood mere feet away from a cliff—the deadly cliff where Chloe had lost her life.

"Let's get out of here."

Thorn nodded, and we made a wide circle around the festival grounds to the road. "You okay?" she asked gently.

"As okay as anyone can be after acting like some kind of one-girl freak show. I can't believe I went up in front of people! What if the reporter filmed me! The last thing I want is to have people know about me—what I can see. But I didn't have control, like I wasn't even me."

"I couldn't believe it when you jumped up and started talking to yourself."

"I was talking to Chloe."

"If you say so," she said doubtfully. "Did she talk back?"

"Yeah, but not aloud the way we're talking. It was like she was inside me. Yet I saw her, too, and felt her emotions."

"She's possessing you?"

"It's more like she's forcing me to help her. Only I'm afraid of what she plans to do. I could have found out more only the lights went on."

"From what I could tell of the angry crowd, the lights were supposed to stay off. Whoever turned them on should have his face smashed."

"Any idea who did it?"

"Beats me." Thorn shrugged, stepping around a deep puddle. "I'm still ticked I couldn't even see the ghost. All I saw on the pavilion was rain, mist, and you. Are you sure you were talking to Chloe?"

"Definitely."

We lapsed into silence as we headed to the car, my emotions raw and anxiety growing. I felt sorry for Chloe; it must be horrible to be trapped in limbo. It was obviously confusing her into paranoid accusations. Was James the betrayer? If so, then why was she still speaking of loving him? She was clearly one messed-up ghost.

Why can't I have a normal life without weird stuff? I thought angrily. *It's like trying to put together a puzzle with half the pieces missing. And I don't know where to look for the missing pieces.*

That night I plugged in my nightlight and sank under my covers, weary and exhausted. I wanted to sink into peaceful oblivion. So I curled deep under the covers and closed my mind to all things mysterious.

"That includes you, Opal," I added in a whisper so I wouldn't wake Thorn.

Don't get uppity with me young miss, came a sharp reply.

"Oh, so now you're around?" I pursed my lips angrily. "Where were you earlier?"

Time and space rules don't apply here, so there's really no answer you could comprehend. Though I'm always close to you.

"So why didn't you help with Chloe?" I demanded silently.

You'll have to be more specific. I'm not all-knowing, although I do possess vast stores of knowledge.

"Why is Chloe bugging me?"

Why not you? You have gifts that can do much good. When a lost soul seeks help, it takes a strong person to put aside fears and offer assistance.

"I don't have time to deal with a psycho ghost. No way am I going to help her get revenge. That's crazy! Besides, I'm going home tomorrow."

Every action you take is your own choice and I will never utter a word to influence your decisions. I won't mention the joy of putting others' needs above your own. Or how the act of offering help unselfishly can be its own reward.

"The only reward I want is my grandmother to be healthy. Which means finding the charms. Tell me where they are and I'll do anything you want."

I cannot tell what I do not know.

"Then I'll find out on my own!" I sat up in bed, punching my pillow. "I don't need you! Just leave me alone!"

The shake of her head held regret. Then her image faded and she was gone.

Fine! She could stay away for all I cared. If she wouldn't do what I wanted, then I wouldn't do what she wanted either. After one more trip to the retirement resort, I was out of here.

Good-bye Pine Peaks.

Good-bye Chloe.

*   *   *

I awoke to sunshine and a refreshing sense of new beginnings, as if last night's rain had washed away all night phantoms. With renewed energy, I slipped into jeans and a sweatshirt. Just a few more hours until I would be back home with Nona, where I belonged. And tonight I'd attend my first dance with Josh.

I was feeling so good, it was a bit of a shock to come downstairs and find Thorn sitting meekly in a chair with her expression downcast and her shoulders hunched. Her aunt stood over her with folded arms and a stern expression. Something was up. And it didn't take long to find out.

"Sabine, please join us," Mrs. Matthews said briskly. "This concerns you, too."

I gulped and shared an uneasy look with Thorn, who twisted her ponytail and had a guilty flush.

"I had a very interesting phone call early this morning." Thorn's aunt pinched her lips together. "Beth, do you remember Mrs. Snope?"

Thorn shook her head.

"Mrs. Snope works at the library. And she remembers you."

"Oh?" Thorn glanced down at the carpet as if the floral pattern was fascinating.

"Mrs. Snope was working late last night. And on her way home, she saw you going into the park. Who exactly was this friend you were visiting?" she asked with suspicious emphasis on the word "visiting."

"Uh . . . you wouldn't know her."

"I'm sure I wouldn't. But I do know your mother wouldn't approve of your being involved in occult activities. She is a minister, after all, and preaches honest beliefs, not ghost chasing."

A minister! I shot Thorn a startled look.

"Beth honey, I'm sure you had a good reason for going to one of those occult gatherings and I want to hear what it is. We've always been honest with each other, I know you wouldn't lie to me."

"I didn't . . . not really . . ." Thorn's words trailed off and she looked so miserable my heart went out to her.

"She didn't lie," I said. "It was all my idea."

"Oh?" Mrs. Matthews's brow raised as she turned her attention to me. "What exactly was your idea?"

"Uh—going to the pavilion." I gulped. "We—uh—we planned to visit a friend, but I wanted to see a ghost. So I convinced Tho—Beth to go there instead."

"I'm sorry, Aunt Deb," Thorn added contritely. With her hair swept back in a ponytail and not a trace of makeup, she looked young and sweet.

"I know you wouldn't intentionally do anything wrong, but I'm responsible for you while you're here and I can't help but worry."

"All we did was get rained on. There wasn't anything to see."

"Of course not," her aunt said with a pragmatic wave of her hand. "It's a lot of nonsense. That's why Charles and I avoid going into town this time of year. Too much traffic and unsavory sorts milling around, not a healthy environment for two innocent girls."

I glanced at Thorn, expecting her to scowl at being called "innocent," but she merely nodded.

"We won't be around much longer anyway," Thorn added. "One more trip out to Peaceful Pines, then we're going home."

Home. I smiled slightly, thinking of Josh, Nona, and Penny-Love. I couldn't wait to get back. In a few hours my life would return to normal. I'd be glad to see Thorn back to normal, too, dressed in black and threatening to smash faces.

After a breakfast of scrambled eggs, sausage, and strawberries, I tried once more to call Nona. But all I got was one of those fast, busy signals. Like the phone was off the hook or out of order. I tried Penny-Love and her mother told me she was off with some friends. *Which friends?* I wondered, feeling a bit left out. I was tempted to call Josh, but it was still early and I knew he liked to sleep in late.

It was also too early to go to the retirement resort, so I went into my room and started packing. I was zipping my toiletry bag when I heard the phone ring from downstairs. A few moments later, Mrs. Matthews peeked into the room and held out a cordless phone to me.

"It's for you. A woman."

"Nona. About time, too." Smiling, I jumped up and reached for the phone.

But it wasn't my grandmother.

"Is this Sabine Rose?" An unfamiliar high-pitched voice asked,

"Yes." Something in her tone made me uneasy. "Who's this?"

"I'm Nurse Eloch from—" Static rippled on the line, making it hard to understand. But my heart lurched when I made out the word "hospital."

"Hospital!" I choked. "What's this about?"

The connection worsened and I had to strain to listen. "I had to—found your number in—"

Her voice flickered in and out. "—trying to contact you—your grandmother."

"What about her?" I demanded, gripping the phone tightly.

"I'm afraid I—bad news."

"About Nona?" My world jolted to a numb stop. "Is she all right?"

"There's been a car accident—" Static interrupted again, garbling her words so all I could make out were, "injuries—come to—hospital."

"Ohmygod! Nona!"

"—intensive care—emergency—not much time—"

"Not much time for what?" I cried. "Speak louder! Tell me what's happened!"

But the static buzzed louder, then a sharp click and a droning dial tone.

The connection went dead.

17

Arms encircled my shoulders and I was faintly aware of someone prying the phone out of my shaking hand. Blinking away tears, I looked up into Mrs. Matthews's concerned face.

"It's going to be all right," she said softly.

"Nona . . . in the hospital." I shook my head, the horrible reality sinking in. "A car accident! I have to go to her!"

"Of course you do, honey. What hospital is she in?"

"I don't know. I got disconnected before I could find out. But it has to be Valley Central, that's the one closest to Nona's house." Hot tears tasted salty on my lips. "Oh, Nona! She has to be okay."

"She will be. You go pack, honey."

Ten minutes later, our suitcases were in the jeep and Thorn was hugging her aunt good-bye. "Tell Uncle Charles good-bye for me," she added.

"I will, honey. You drive carefully and call me when you get there."

Thorn nodded, while I stood there limply, my eyes stinging as I fought to stay in control. Nona needed me to be strong. I couldn't let her down.

"She's going to be all right," Mrs. Matthews assured as she waved from the doorstep.

"I hope so," I said through a fog.

"You're welcome to come back here anytime. We've loved having you visit."

"Thank you . . . thanks for everything." My voice broke and I turned away.

The jeep roared to life with a jolt and I grabbed the armrest. But I still felt off-balance, my heart racing faster than the jeep. I glanced at my watch, calculating how long it would take to get home. Too long—not fast enough. *Oh, Nona, I'm coming.*

Thorn reached over to squeeze my hand. "Take it easy, Sabine."

"This is all my fault. I never should have left her."

"She's a grown woman. You're not her babysitter."

"But I should have known something bad would happen."

"Why?" Thorn asked, her eyes widening. "Did you have a premonition?"

"No. I almost never get them for people close to me. And all this Chloe drama confuses things. But I've had a bad feeling. Nona hasn't answered the phone and I've worried about her memory problems. And now—now she's hurt—maybe dying." The sick pit of fear in my gut hurt so badly, I could hardly breathe. If anything bad happened to my grandmother, I'd never forgive myself. Never.

"She's going to be fine," Thorn assured. "Think positively."

"Yeah." But the image that flashed through my head was of Nona pale and stiff in a hospital bed. Was this a premonition or just my own fears?

Thorn slowed as the long private road ended at the main highway. She flipped on her left blinker and waited for an opening in the busy traffic. I stared numbly out the window. The sky was blue and serene, opposite of the dark and stormy fears rushing through me.

Someone started honking and Thorn raised her fist toward the rearview mirror. "What's that idiot doing?" she exclaimed angrily.

"Huh? What?" I asked numbly.

"Some jerk just zoomed by, then spun a U-ie and is now honking at us."

I lifted my head and glanced over my shoulder. My vision was blurry and I vaguely made out a white truck. The honking grew louder, more insistent. There wasn't anything unusual about it, yet something made me sit up straight and look closer.

"I'll show that creep he can't mess with us," Thorn raged. "That beat-up metal monster can't keep up with me. Get ready to eat my dust!"

"No, Thorn!" I shook my head urgently. "Pull over!"

"What? I'm not stopping for that jerk."

"He's not a jerk—well, at least not all the time." I pointed out the window. "It's Dominic."

*　　　*　　　*

Dominic wore dark jeans, a brown shirt, and grass-stained work boots. A breeze blew his sandy-brown hair and his tanned, muscular arms were taut with energy as he slammed his truck door and strode over. "Took you long enough to stop," he said, scowling. "I drive all this way to help you search and then see you driving—hey, what's wrong?"

"Don't you know?" My voice broke off.

"Know what?"

"About the accident!"

"What accident? Are you okay?" he asked with a sudden shift from rough to gentle that broke something in me and tears clouded my eyes.

"Not me—it's Nona."

I turned away so he wouldn't see me cry. I hated myself for losing it, even though I knew Dominic would understand because he cared about Nona, too. While I fought to hold myself together,

Thorn quickly filled Dominic in on the phone call from the hospital.

"So we're headed there now," Thorn added. "You can follow us."

"I don't think so," he said with a stubborn jut of his jaw.

"Why not?"

"Because I just talked to Nona on the phone."

I stared at him. "Impossible!"

"There was no car accident." He shook his head gravely. "Whoever called you was lying."

18

At first I didn't believe Dominic. Then when he pulled out a cell phone, I nearly fell over at the sound of Nona's voice, strong and well! I wasn't sure whether I was more shocked to find out she was fine or discover that loner Dominic had his own cell phone.

"Hi, honey," Nona said calmly. "How are you doing?"

"How am *I* doing? You want to know how *I'm* doing!" I started laughing and crying at the same time.

"Sabine, what's wrong?" her voice rose with alarm. "Are you in some kind of trouble?"

"Not me. But I thought you were. I tried to call and no one answered and then the line was busy. Why couldn't I get through?"

"You know how bad the lines get when it rains, and the phone was out all yesterday."

"All day?" I rubbed my aching head.

"It's still out. I've had a devil of a time running my business with only this cell phone I borrowed from Penny-Love. Thank goodness for her! She truly is a love and offered the use of her laptop. She had such clever ideas for getting new clients that I may offer her a part-time job."

I shook my head, trying to make sense of everything. But I was so overwhelmed with relief that I could hardly think. Thank God Nona was okay! Imagining her hurt or worse had been a nightmare. I never wanted to go through that again. I couldn't stand to lose her. And I'd do anything, no matter what it took, to find the missing remedy book.

When I finished talking to Nona, I handed the phone back to Dominic. "Thanks," I told him, only dimly aware of cars whizzing past as we stood on the side of the road.

"No problem." He shrugged.

"If you hadn't stopped us, we'd still be on our way to the hospital." I shuddered. "How did you know?"

"I didn't. But I was on my way to see you and recognized the yellow jeep."

"No one can miss it," Thorn said wryly. "I better call my aunt and uncle to let them know your grandmother is okay."

"Here. Use this." Dominic offered his phone.

When Thorn stepped away to make her call, Dominic turned to me with a puzzled arch of his dark brows. "What's with her new look?" he asked, gesturing toward Thorn.

I wrinkled my brow, then smiled when I realized what he meant. "Oh, her hair and clothes. She's taking a Goth break."

He frowned. "Too bad."

"Why? You prefer the dark, diva look?"

"On her I do. It's honest."

"You think she's more honest when she's wearing chains and a wig?"

"It's who she is. Deep, dark, and complex."

"And what about me?" I wanted to slap myself the moment I asked this. What was I thinking? I sounded like one of those phony flirts who played guys, fishing for complements and acting all superficial. Yet when he didn't answer right away, I felt anxious. What did he think of me? And why did I even care?

"I don't know about you—yet," Dominic finally said, leaning so close that my breath caught. The way he added "yet" was part threat, part promise. He reached out and lightly touched the black streak flowing in my blond hair.

For a moment, our eyes met. I could hardly breathe. Emotions flowed over me, hot and volatile, like I was standing still under a volcano. The intensity scared me, and quickly I turned away to see if Thorn was finished with her call. Nope. Still talking.

When I found the courage to glance back at Dominic, he had slipped on his sunglasses, hiding behind dark lenses.

"So how goes the investigation?" he asked in a casual tone.

"Slow." Deep breath. Act normal. "We went to see Eleanor Baskers yesterday—she's a descendent of the woman who took care of Agnes's daughters. So there's a chance she knows what happened to the sisters and the charms. But when we went to see her, she wasn't there. Thorn and I were getting ready to try again today—until we got that call about Nona."

"Any idea who called?"

"None." Nervously, I rattled on, "I guess I could have heard wrong. It was a bad connection with a lot of static. But I'm sure she said that Nona had been in a car accident. Maybe she had me mixed up with someone else."

"Doubtful."

"Yeah, she knew my name," I remembered. "She said she was a nurse... yeah, Nurse Eloch."

"From what hospital?" he asked.

"I don't know. If she told me, I couldn't hear. The connection kept breaking up. But Nona is fine, so I guess it doesn't matter now."

"It matters," he said with a fierce expression. "Making a call like that is criminal."

"It has to be a mistake."

"Or a deliberate attempt to stop you from seeing Eleanor Baskers."

"You can't be serious! That's crazy."

"There are a lot of crazies out there."

I nodded, thinking of Chloe and her obsessed fans. "Still, why would anyone want to stop me from helping my grandmother? That's just cruel."

"People are cruel," he said bluntly.

"Maybe it's not about Nona—but the missing charms. Is it possible someone else is searching for them, too?"

"Anything's possible."

"Well no one is going to stop me from finding them," I said with growing determination. "Thorn and I will go right to Peaceful Pines Resort."

"So will I." He reached into his pocket and pulled out his car keys. "See you there."

Without asking if we minded his going, he climbed into his truck and the door shut with a sharp bang. His engine roared and the stench of diesel gas made my nose scrunch. Gravel spurted with dust as he roared away.

"Where's he off to?" Thorn asked, rushing over to my side and cupping her hand over her eyes as she gazed after him. "He didn't wait to get his cell phone."

"You'll see him soon enough anyway. He's headed for Peaceful Pines."

"Ahead of us?" Thorn complained. "Come on, let's get moving."

We hurried into the yellow jeep and headed for Peaceful Pines. Unfortunately that meant going through Pine Peaks. As we neared town, cars increased and traffic slowed to a turtle's crawl. The banner announcing the Chloe Celebration waved cheerfully overhead as we inched into downtown.

"Not again." Thorn slapped her palm against the steering wheel. "I hate traffic jams."

"Look on the bright side. If we're stuck, so is Dominic."

"Good point. Still traffic sucks. It'll take an hour to drive five miles at this rate." Thorn pressed on her horn and gave an impatient beep. "Hey, move it already gray car."

"There's a line of cars in front of him," I told her. "Be patient."

"But I'm not patient. I will be so glad to get home where I can be myself again."

"Put on your black wig if it'll make you feel better."

"And risk Mrs. Snope or some other nosy friend of my aunt's ratting on me? I can put up with this look for a few more hours." Then she blasted the horn again.

My gaze wandered out the window and I noticed a TV crew. My first impulse was to duck down low in case the camera focused on the traffic. But when I noticed the slim older woman being interviewed by Heidi, I watched curiously.

"Hey, Thorn." I nudged her in mid-honk. "That's Cathy, the cotton-candy-haired woman I met yesterday."

"The ghost's best friend?"

"Yeah. She's probably telling Heidi the same story she told me."

"Getting her fifteen minutes of fame," Thorn said with a snort.

"I bet she gets more than fifteen minutes. She told me they used to call her and Chloe the 'Stormy C's' because they were so wild."

"Everything's wild in a town that celebrates a ghost." Thorn pointed across the street. "Check out that guy wearing a tin-foil hat."

"Major weird," I said, swiveling to look. "But he's got it all wrong. Foil hats ward off aliens, not ghosts."

"Did your grandmother tell you about aliens, too?"

"No," I said with a laugh. "I saw it on a Mel Gibson movie."

Amazingly, traffic started to move and minutes later we turned on the rural road leading to Peaceful Pines. It was bumpier than before, rutted with muddy puddles.

The sun had vanished; gray clouds swirled with gusty winds as we pulled into Peaceful Pines's parking lot. I spotted Dominic's truck, only he wasn't in it. When I looked over at the office, I saw the door closing behind him.

"Good!" I said with satisfaction. "While he's with the manager, we can get to Eleanor first. He'll have to wait for Mrs. Fontaine's dog to stop barking before he can find out which cottage is Eleanor's. But we already know."

I shut the jeep door behind me, then led Thorn through the parking lot and beyond the clubhouse. We followed the path to the cozy, white cottages, each separated by a small yard and neatly manicured patch of lawn. I read cottage numbers until I came to Number 261.

But the building was dark and no one answered the door.

"Knock louder," Thorn suggested. "Mrs. Baskers could be hard of hearing or in the shower."

"Or still in Florida," came a sarcastic voice behind me and I turned to find Dominic standing there with an amused smile.

"How do you know?"

"The manager told me there's a hurricane warning so the plane was delayed again."

"Are you sure?" I said with sinking discouragement. "If that dog was yapping the whole time, you might have heard wrong."

"Yes, I'm sure," Dominic replied. "And the dog only yaps because he hates prissy haircuts."

Thorn tilted her head at him. "So you're a dog expert?"

"No," he replied with a closed expression.

"He has a special way with animals," I said vaguely. I knew about Dominic's ability to communicate with animals, but had promised to keep it a secret. So I ignored Thorn's questioning gaze and turned back to Dominic. "Did the manager say when Mrs. Baskers would return?"

"She hopes to catch a flight out in the morning."

"Which means she won't be here until tomorrow night! But I can't stay that long." I groaned, thinking of my plans to help Penny-Love decorate for the dance and my date with Josh.

"You go back home and I'll finish up here," Dominic said. I knew I should be grateful for his offer, but I wasn't ready to leave yet.

I didn't say much as we left the cottage, instead I argued back and forth with my conscience. I'd been looking forward to this dance, eager to show off my decorating creativity. Also, there was Josh, who was so hot other girls envied me for dating him. This would be our first appearance as a couple and I couldn't wait to dance with him.

But then I thought of my grandmother. She trusted me to find the remedy. There would be other dances, but there was only one Nona.

I was about to tell Thorn my decision to stay, but as we returned to the parking lot, she suddenly screamed. Horror played on her face and she ran forward.

Dominic and I exchanged a surprised look, then raced after her. We caught up with Thorn by her yellow jeep. With her mouth open in shock, she pointed to her jeep.

The canvas top was cut to ribbons, the tires were slashed, and the windshield was cracked. As we ran up for a closer look, I saw a sheet of paper on the seatback of the driver's seat.

It was held in place with a huge knife.

19

Dominic pulled a rag from his pocket and carefully pried the knife out of the seat. With a solemn nod, he handed the note to Thorn.

She took one look, went a shade paler, and then handed it to me. The message was short, printed in thick black ink: "Leave town or die."

"Who would do such a thing?" I exclaimed, my hands shaking as I read the note again.

Thorn shook her head.

"I don't get it," I said in a feeble attempt to act calm and not panic. Still, it was hard to ignore a death threat. "Why would anyone want us to leave? Is this some sick joke?"

"Nothing funny about that knife," Thorn said with a shudder.

"Or this note," Dominic said solemnly. "Any idea who left it?"

"None," I answered. "First the phone call and now this. It's more than a coincidence. Someone is trying to scare us away."

"A note doesn't scare me, but my mother does." Thorn rubbed her forehead. "When she sees her jeep, she's gonna kill me."

"This isn't your fault," I said. "Besides, isn't it your mother's job to be forgiving?"

"Not when it comes to her car. I'd rather take my chances with the sicko." Thorn sagged against the door and rubbed her forehead. "I'll have to report this to the insurance company or the police."

"Then we'd be stuck here for hours filling out papers and answering questions," Dominic pointed out.

"And the sicko wins because we'll have to leave town without talking to Eleanor Baskers," I added glumly.

"Do you think that's what this is about?" Thorn asked. "Someone wants to prevent us from talking to Mrs. Baskers?"

"Well it isn't going to work because I'm not giving up," I vowed.

"But what about my jeep?" Thorn asked, spreading out her hands in a frustrated gesture. "How am I going to fix it?"

"Leave it to me." Dominic stepped forward. He went around to the bed of his truck and came back with a plastic bag. Carefully, he placed the knife in the bag. Then he offered to handle the repairs to Thorn's car.

"Since when do you know about cars?" I faced him with my hands on my hips. "I thought you only knew about animals."

"Stick around and learn more." With a wink, he turned and pulled out his cell phone.

While he was talking to some "pal" in the auto business, I studied him. Why did he make me feel so uneasy? He'd been nothing but helpful, yet I still didn't feel comfortable around him. Like there was something unspoken between us.

Frustrated, I turned away and glanced around over at the clubhouse. The large picture window offered a clear view of the lot. Had someone inside witnessed the vandalism?

Dominic was still talking on the phone, pausing now and then to ask Thorn questions about her car. They didn't notice when I slipped away to the clubhouse.

When I entered the overly warm, stuffy room, I was disappointed to find it nearly deserted. The TV was off and there weren't any card players. A hunched man sat at a chair near the window, which would have given him a clear view of the parking lot. Only as I started toward him, I saw his white cane and the Braille book he was touch reading. The only other people around were two women chatting as they crocheted and a silverhaired man working a crossword puzzle. But none of them were anywhere near the window.

Discouraged, I turned to leave, until my gaze fell on the man quietly working a crossword puzzle. He wore a jaunty naval cap with impressive emblems—the sort a retired admiral might wear. Curiously, I stepped closer.

He looked about old enough to be Chloe's fiancé. And his blue-and-dark-orange aura vibrated with a strong sense of strength and confidence. But how could I find out for sure? You just didn't walk up to a stranger and ask him if he'd been engaged to a ghost.

While I tried to come up with a good opening, he swiveled in his chair to look directly at me. "Young woman, if you have business to discuss, please state it swiftly and succinctly so I can go on with my crossword. I find being stared at quite disconcerting."

"I didn't mean to stare," I said with a flush.

"The most well-meaning individuals are usually the most intrusive."

"I'm sorry . . . but are you Theodore?"

"Retired Admiral Theodore Alexander Viscente or Teddy to my friends," he said in a clipped tone. His blue eyes were faded with age, but there was a sharpness to his gaze that made me lift my shoulders and snap to attention. "I don't believe we've met."

"I heard about you." I clasped my hands. "Weren't you engaged once to Chloe . . . the ghost?"

"Humph! All this ghost nonsense is an insult to her memory." He tapped so hard on his pencil the lead point broke. "As a rule, I don't discuss her, but I'm tired of how this town glorified her death rather than her short life. She was a beautiful, sweet girl and if she hadn't died tragically, she would have been my wife."

"It must have been really hard for you," I said sympathetically.

"It's been over fifty years, water under this old bridge. Life goes on."

"But you must have loved her deeply."

"She was the only one for me and always will be." He paused to regard me sharply. "So why the third degree? You're too young to be with the media."

I bristled at being called too young, but hid my annoyance with a shrug. "I'm just curious about Chloe."

"A lot more than curiosity brought you all the way out here. Most folks in Pine Peaks tend to forget we old geezers exist."

"I'm just visiting. I had hoped to see Eleanor Baskers—she's a. . . relative—only she isn't back yet. I read Chloe's biography, and I'm surprised there's no mention of your engagement."

"That book is full of inaccuracies. Any fool can write a book, and Kasper has to be the biggest idiot I've ever met. An outsider like him has no right to present himself as the authority on Chloe. He never even met her."

"But he knows all about ghosts," I said.

"So he's a nutcase like the others who flock here every October. What a lot of rot." He snorted with disgust. "If ghosts were real, don't you think Chloe would have shown herself to me?"

"Well—I guess."

"Of course she would. I was very close to her parents, too and I have yet to be visited by their ghosts. They treated me like a son and there wasn't anything I wouldn't do for them."

"Then why was the engagement a secret?"

"It wasn't my idea, I assure you." He folded the corner of his crossword puzzle page with his gnarled hands. "Chloe was full of spirit and not in a rush to settle down. So we agreed to wait until after her graduation before formally announcing our engagement. But before that could happen. . ." His hands dropped to his sides.

"She died," I finished sadly.

He lifted his head with a challenging gaze. "I suppose you believe the stories about her falling for a stranger and planning to run away with him?"

"Isn't that what happened?"

"More rot and rubbish."

"She didn't fall in love with James?"

"Chloe had many admirers. She was so beautiful, you only had to look at her to fall in love. She may have danced with James, but I was the man she planned to marry. He meant nothing to her."

"So you knew him?"

"No. I wasn't much of a dancer and never went to the pavilion. But I was told he only stayed a short time." Theodore's lips pressed into a thin line. "No one knows where he went, but good riddance. He deserved whatever he got."

"What do you think happened to him?" I asked with a shiver.

"I have no idea, nor do I care. Don't believe everything you hear or read about Chloe. Only those truly close to her know the truth." He wagged his finger at me, then scribbled an answer in his puzzle.

But what was the truth? I wondered as I slowly walked away. My dream of Chloe replayed in my mind. She'd looked so radiant as she danced in James's arms. I sensed her excitement and passion. Chloe may have been engaged to Theodore, but it was James that she loved.

Had James loved her back? What had they argued about on the cliff? Or had that been someone else with her? What did it all mean?

I wasn't sure if James stood Chloe up or somehow caused her death. But the one fact that seemed clear was that James had vanished that night, too. Why hadn't anyone ever heard from him again? Chloe seemed to think he was still around, and maybe she was right. An ugly suspicion twisted like a knife in my soul.

Had James really left that fateful night? I wondered. *Or was he buried nearby in an unmarked grave? Had James been murdered?*

20

"What are you doing?" I asked Thorn when I returned to the jeep and saw her cradling the knife in her hands, staring down with zombie-like concentration. Her eyes were half-closed, unblinking, and her aura shimmered lavender and silver.

"*Shhhh*," Dominic cautioned, putting his finger to his lips as he came up beside me. "Don't startle her. She's been like that for ten minutes."

I nodded with understanding. "She's finding."

Leaning against the jeep with his arms folded, Dominic regarded me curiously. "How does it work?"

"She touches something and gets mental pictures about it."

"Like your visions?"

"Not really. I get confusing glimpses of the past or future and I have no control when it'll happen. But Thorn can get vibes on almost anything she focuses on."

"Oh," he said with a nod. "Psychometry."

"How'd you know about that?"

"Library books. I read a lot."

"You do?"

"Don't look so shocked."

"I'm not. It's just that you're always working outside."

"A guy has to work all his muscles. Including this one." Dominic tapped his head, smiling as if he enjoyed surprising me.

And I was surprised, but not because he was smart. I already knew that. What I hadn't expected was how his smile warmed me. And the fresh scent of his hair reminded me of wild grasses deep in the woods. A sandy blond curl stuck out unevenly by his ear and I had the urge to smooth it. Instead, I self-consciously smoothed my own hair.

He glanced expectantly at me, as if waiting. For what? I had no idea. Instead, I turned toward Thorn who was still transfixed on the knife.

Dominic followed my gaze. "How long does she usually take?" he asked.

"I don't know. I've only seen her do this a few times."

"As long as it works." He walked over to the jeep and ran his hand over the punctured canvas top. "I want to find the jerk who did this."

"Me, too. It's creepy having an unknown enemy."

"Don't let him scare you. Only cowards leave threats."

I nodded, but I was still uneasy. This note brought back ugly memories from last year at Arcadia High—when everyone turned against me after that boy died. My locker was vandalized, the tires of my bike slashed, and I'd gotten notes far worse than this. I'd thought all the hate and fear was behind me, but I'd already made an enemy in Evan Marshall and now this note. A subtle enemy was far more dangerous. Not knowing who to watch out for put me on edge.

"Glass." Thorn broke the silence, suddenly lifting her head up. "Shiny glass."

Dominic and I rushed over to her.

"What did you see?" I gently laid my hand on Thorn's shoulder.

"The knife surrounded by glass . . .on display, I think, in a case."

"Where?" Dominic asked.

Thorn blinked. "A glass shelf—no, a counter-top with a lot of people—near a cash register."

"A store?" Dominic guessed.

"Yeah, that's right. I can see the building even—it's brick and there's a velvet painting of dogs on the wall. It feels close." Excitedly, Thorn grabbed Dominic's hand. "Let's take your truck."

Most guys would have asked more questions, but Dominic seemed to get it. Without hesitation, he whipped out his keys and led us to his truck. After buckling up, he turned to Thorn for directions.

"That way," Thorn said, cradling the knife in one hand while pointing with the other. Energy sizzled from her, as if she was on fire inside.

Gloomy clouds had rolled into Pine Peaks and a brisk wind scuttled brittle leaves across pavement. Skeletal trees lining Main Street were as bare as the sidewalks, making the usually bustling town seem eerie and deserted.

We easily found a parking space in front of a sporting store called The Great Outdoors. Hunting supplies crowded a window display—camouflage jackets, sturdy boots, bows and arrows, and razor-edged knives. Although this store was the most logical destination, Thorn shook her head like a sleepwalker and continued down the sidewalk, clutching a bag containing the knife. We passed Bubba's Barbershop, High Peaks Realtors, Tansy's Trinkets, The Chloe Museum, and Glittermania before Thorn led us inside a square, brick store called Golden Oldies.

"Here?" Dominic and I looked at a display window with knickknacks and a mannequin sporting stylish secondhand clothes.

"Yeah," Thorn seemed to lose her energy and sank down in a bench on the sidewalk. "I need to sit for a minute. Go inside and look for a glass case of jewelry and old coins."

"We'll be right back," I told her.

Dominic nodded, then we pushed through the wood door.

A clerk wearing a diamond in her belly button and low-riding jeans noticed us right away. Or more accurately—she noticed Dominic. The badge on her vest identified her as Assistant Manager, Tawnya.

"Hi there," she said with a smile that widened as she checked him out. "What can I do for *you*?"

Dominic lifted the knife from the bag and laid it on the glass counter. "We found this on the sidewalk in front of your store."

"No kidding?" Her eyes widened. "Usually tourists just lose keys. First time anyone's lost a knife."

"You recognize it?" he said, pointing to the golden hilt and sharp silver blade.

"It looks familiar—but *you* don't. I remember all my interesting customers." She leaned across the counter, all smiley and fluttery lashes, reminding me of a sleek feline on the prowl. "You here for the celebration?"

"Uh . . ." He paused, then nodded. "Yeah."

"Figures," she said as if disappointed. "Another ghost chaser. Around here Chloe is like an

American Idol. I used to be a fan, too, but that was before—"

"About this knife." Dominic interrupted. "Any idea who owns it?"

"I have an idea who used to own it."

"Who?" I asked.

She ignored me, totally focused on Dominic as she ran her finger over the knife's hilt. "See this tiny *R* etched into the handle? Means it's from the Rafferty Estate. But he died and we sold his stuff months ago."

"Can you find out who bought this?"

"Our records aren't open to the public."

"Oh," Dominic said disappointed.

She winked at him. "But I can check—for you."

Dominic's face reddened. "Uh . . . thanks."

"No prob. I'm happy to serve my customers." She fluttered her purple, glittered lashes, smiling at Dominic in a flirty way that made me want to gag. Could she be more obvious?

She never stopped ogling Dominic as she booted up a computer. "Yeah, it was from the Rafferty estate and sold over five months ago."

"That long?" Dominic knitted his brows. "Who bought it?"

"No way of telling since they paid cash. Records only show date sold and items purchased."

"What else was bought?" he asked.

"Weird stuff." She tapped a pink-tipped fingernail on the computer screen. "A fake fur rug, goldfish bowl, and a size-six ladies' shoe."

"Only one shoe?" Dominic raised his brows.

"Maybe someone with only one leg. If I find out more, I'll let you know. Leave me your number." She paused to look at me for the first time. "That is, if your girlfriend doesn't mind."

"I'm not his—I mean—"

Dominic patted my arm affectionately. "She doesn't mind."

My face flamed and I lost the ability to speak. Why didn't he correct her? How could anyone think we were dating?

But Dominic simply pulled a pen from his pocket and jotted down his number. She picked up the paper with a sly smile, and then she turned to me. "Hope you know how lucky you are."

"Oh, I know all right." I shot Dominic an annoyed look.

"You've got a great guy here."

"Yeah, just great."

My sarcasm seemed lost on Tawyna. Instead, an odd look crossed her face and she gestured for me to come closer. "Can we talk for a moment alone?" she asked. "There's something you need to know."

"Uh . . . sure." Puzzled, I glanced at Dominic. He shrugged, then offered to step outside.

"I've got to warn you," Tawyna spoke in a hushed tone. "About the celebration tonight."

"What about it?"

"You should talk your boyfriend out of going."

I started to set her straight about Dominic and our relationship, but the anxiety in her tone changed my mind. I'd find out more by saying less. "Why?"

"It's not safe for cute guys. If he goes, watch out for him. He reminds me of my ex-boyfriend Leon and that could mean trouble if he gets near the ghost."

"What do you mean?"

"Chloe has everyone fooled, but I know she's dangerous."

My heart quickened. "How?"

"Because of Leon. He was a Chloe fan, too—until she tried to kill him."

21

The store's door banged shut and a chilly wind whipped around me. As I struggled to tame my hair, I heard a crinkling sound and glanced up at the "Chloe Celebration" banner. Wind-torn and ragged, it flapped overhead like a battered bird.

I expected to find Dominic and Thorn on the bench, but it was empty. I glanced around and spotted them in Dominic's truck.

As I crossed the street, I couldn't stop thinking about Chloe. Was she a tragic victim or a dangerous spirit? According to Tawyna, the ghost lured her ex-boyfriend to an isolated cliff. He grew dizzy, like he was in a trance. Then he stumbled as if someone pushed him and he started to fall over the cliff. If he hadn't grabbed onto an old tree, he would have died. His friends finally heard his frantic shouts, but no one believed a ghost attacked him. They accused him of drinking too much and being clumsy.

Tawyna admitted that he *was* clumsy and he *did* drink too much. But she believed his story. I wasn't sure if I did—but I wouldn't forget it. Was he the guy I'd seen falling in my dream vision? The more I found out about Chloe, the sooner I wanted to leave town.

A short while later, Dominic was talking to a mechanic, a thirty-something guy with a long skinny beard and the odd nickname of "Goat," who agreed to pick up Thorn's jeep and have it repaired by tomorrow morning.

I glanced at my watch and groaned. Almost three already. There was no way I'd make it back in time for the dance. With a sigh, I went to make two calls.

"Sabine, it's about time!" Penny-Love said when she heard my voice. "I was beginning to think you'd never call. I was starting to worry."

"Nothing to worry about, I'm fine."

"It's the dance I'm worried about! I have boxes of ribbons, streamers, and paint, but zero talent for decorating."

"Anyone can twist crepe paper and put up banners."

"Not me. I'm counting on you to help me whip up some awesome decorations. You were due back yesterday."

"Sorry. Things got crazy." It would be easier if I could be completely honest. But explaining about my gift was tricky. My last best friend turned against me when she found out. So I was in no hurry to tell Penny-Love.

"Things are way more crazy here," Penny-Love went on in her usual overly dramatic way. She may have some faults, but being boring was not one of them. "I've been stressing over the dance, going to cheer practice, doing tons of homework, and helping your grandmother. Did you hear about her losing electricity and how I loaned her my laptop?"

"Yeah, she told me. Thanks for helping her."

"It was fun. I'll tell you all about it in person as soon as you get your butt to my house. We've got tons to do. How soon can you come over?"

"Well. . . ." I bit my lip. "It could take a while."

"Where exactly are you?"

"Uh . . . in Pine Peaks. And it gets worse." I blew out a heavy sigh and admitted I wasn't returning till tomorrow.

Her shriek was so loud my ears stung. "I can't believe you're doing this to me!"

"I'm sorry. It's just that nothing's worked out right. The family friend I came to see still isn't back yet and Thorn's car needed repairs—"

"Thorn!" Penny-Love cried accusingly. "What does that Goth loser have to do with anything?"

"She's not a loser," I defended. "And she was nice enough to drive me."

"You could have refused. Obviously you'd rather be with her than me."

"No, that's not true—"

"Prove it. Come home now."

"I can't. You don't understand—"

"Oh, I understand perfectly now. You're blowing me off. And I thought you were my friend. Guess I was wrong." When she slammed the phone in my ear, the sharp click slammed into my heart.

I deserve that, I thought miserably. She'd counted on me, and I let her down.

Unfortunately, I had one more person to let down.

Maybe Josh won't be home, I hoped as the phone rang a second, then a third time. He's probably out shooting hoops with Zach or at one of those secret magician meetings. It'll be easier to leave a message. It'll give me time to come up with a good explanation and for him to cool off.

But Josh answered on the fifth ring.

"Sabine!" He sounded so happy to hear from me that I felt even worse.

"Hey," I said feebly.

"So how was your trip?"

"Okay . . . just longer than I expected." Before I chickened out, I sucked in a deep breath and told him I was still in Pine Peaks. Then I braced myself.

Only Josh didn't yell or even hang up. Instead he said something that cut sharper, deeper than the knife that sliced through Thorn's jeep. And I was the one who ended up angry—and hurt—because Josh was still going to the dance. Without me.

But that wasn't the worst part.

Before Josh hung up, he told me he was hanging out with Evan again. Evan Marshall—living up to his "Moving on Marsh" reputation—has moved on from Shelby. He was going to the dance with a new girlfriend from a Bay-area school. I didn't recognize her name, but I nearly died when Josh told me what school she attended: Arcadia High—my old school.

If Evan didn't already know my secret, he would soon.

Then he'd destroy me.

22

As Dominic drove us back to Thorn's aunt and uncle's, I stared out the window at skeletal trees and infinite darkness. I thought back to when I'd first started dating Josh. I'd been noticing him since I arrived at Sheridan, but never had the courage to talk to him. Then suddenly he was in trouble and my sixth sense warned me in time to help. He'd been more than grateful—actually interested in me. And just like that we were going out.

I was so proud to have such a cool guy interested in me. My girlfriends congratulated me and said I was so lucky. But tonight girls would line up to dance with Josh. And when he dumped me, no one would think I was lucky.

Penny-Love was so mad she'd never speak to me again. And after Evan found out, and told what happened at my last school, I'd lose the rest of my friends. Well, except for Manny and Thorn.

"You okay?" Dominic asked softly as he spun the steering wheel. I sat beside him while Thorn listened to her headphones in the backseat. "Don't let that note worry you."

"It's not the note."

"Then what?"

I shook my head. "Nothing."

"You didn't get bad news about Nona?"

"Just what we already know. Otherwise, she's great."

"But you're not," he accused.

I didn't answer and shut him out by facing the window. Dominic wouldn't think missing a dance was a big deal. He didn't seem to need friends or care what anyone thought of him. I doubted he'd ever gone to a school dance. I wasn't even sure he'd attended school. I knew a little about his past, that his mother was dead and he'd had a rough time with an abusive uncle. Otherwise, he was a mystery.

As we neared our turn off, Thorn took off her headphones and made arrangements with Dominic for getting the jeep in the morning. When she asked where he was staying the night, he said he was camping out. "No better ceiling than stars and sky," he added.

After he dropped us off, I told Thorn I wasn't feeling well and went directly to my room. I didn't bother to turn on the light. With the shades drawn, the room was pitch dark. If only I could shut out my feelings so easily. But images kept spinning in my head of Josh, Evan, Penny-Love, Nona, my mother, my sisters, and hostile classmates from Arcadia High.

Did I have some fatal gene that turned people away? Why was my life so complicated? I worked so hard to be what everyone expected that I wasn't sure who I was. If only I could be totally honest. But if I told Penny-Love about Nona's illness and my connection to the other side, would she still want to be my friend? Maybe. But nothing would be normal between us again.

And what about Josh? He hadn't gotten upset when I said I couldn't make the dance. If he really cared, he would have sounded mad or disappointed. Instead he just told me to have fun and said he was only going because he promised to set up the disc jockey equipment for his friend Zach, who was the DJ. And Josh never broke a promise.

I admired Josh's sense of honor. Truly, I did. But I hated him going to a dance without me. What would my friends think? That we'd broken up? Would other girls zero in on Josh? If they asked him to dance, he'd be too polite to refuse. And Evan would be nearby spreading his own poisonous revenge.

Staring up at the ceiling, I was overwhelmed by conflicting emotions—numb yet aching, feeling nothing and everything. I was grateful for my sixth sense when it helped people, but I hated it for making me different. Right now more than anything, I'd rather be at home organizing decorations for the dance.

I'd made a mess of everything. Nona's illness would worsen if I didn't find the remedy book, my mother didn't want me at my sisters' party, Josh was going to the dance without me, Evan was plotting revenge, and I'd let down Penny-Love.

My head ached and I shut my eyes, blinking away tears.

Darkness closed in and I escaped into dreams. . .

*　　*　　*

"Chloe, you can't elope! You're too young!"

"Keep your voice down, Cathy. And help me shut my suitcase."

"You can't do this," Cathy warned, but Chloe hopped on top of the bulging suitcase, then snapped it shut.

"Your parents will just come after you."

"Let them try!" Chloe said with high confidence. "James and I will be long gone before they even notice I'm missing. We'll get married and move to Hollywood. He knows important people who can help me become an actress. At last I'll be a star! My name will be in lights and everyone will admire me."

"People already admire you."

"The boys do, but the girls are too jealous. Except you, which is sweet." She hugged Cathy. *"James is sweet, too, and I can't wait to see him again. I'm sorry about Teddy, but my parents pushed me into that engagement. After I marry James, they can't tell me what to do."*

"You've always done what you wanted anyway."

"True, but they don't know that," she said, giggling. *"If my parents had their way, I'd stay locked away in my room until I was eighteen, then I'd have a dozen kids with boring Teddy and rot in this small town. If it weren't for my secret escape window, I'd never have met James."*

"Teddy is a great catch. Are you sure you don't want him?"

"As a friend only." She waved her hand. *"You can have him."*

"But he doesn't want me." Cathy spoke wistfully, her eyes clouding over. *"You shouldn't have led him on. He's going to be hurt when you leave."*

"It's his own fault for believing I'd ever marry a fuddy-duddy like him. Jeepers, he doesn't have any backbone. He'll end up selling furniture like all the men in his family."

"There's nothing wrong with selling furniture."

"Except that Teddy truly wants to join the Navy. Only he'll never have the courage to stand up to his father. But I have plenty of courage to go after my dreams. James is my dashing prince and this princess is long due for a rescue."

"You should slow down and find out more about James. Where does he come from? What's his family like? You barely know him."

"I know that he loves me."

"But can you trust him?"

"I'm trusting him with my whole future."

"You shouldn't . . . you can't! He's a liar."

"Cathy! What are you saying?"

"The truth. I didn't want to hurt you, but there's no other way. Chloe, there's something I have to tell you about James. . . ."

* * *

Bolting up in bed, I stared around the dark, unfamiliar room, not sure where I was or even who I was. Blackness swallowed me whole, and I fought against panic. Even after I plugged in my night-light, surrounding myself in an angel's glow, my heart still raced. I had the eerie feeling of traveling a long distance. I was back now . . . but not alone.

Although I couldn't see Chloe, in some mysterious way, our destinies were entwined. She was giving me clues about her past that were impossible to ignore. Even if I left Pine Peaks, she'd continue to haunt my dreams.

She needed my help and I needed to help her. I only hoped no one got hurt.

23

I reread the note I'd just written:

Thorn,
Went with Dominic. Back in a few hours.
Will explain everything later.

I stared at my message, then decided it needed more. So I added: *Your friend, Sabine.* Then I left the note on Thorn's pillow, grabbed my jacket, and left the room. I crept silently down the hall, pausing to listen into the family room where Thorn watched a movie with her aunt and uncle. Then I slipped out the back door.

When I'd called Dominic and asked for a ride to the ghost festival, he hadn't sounded surprised. In fact, I'd been the one surprised when he'd not only agreed to take me, but to go along, too. I wasn't sure if this was a good idea, not after Tawnya's bizarre warning, but I kept these thoughts to myself.

Hearing the roar of a diesel pickup, I hurried down the long driveway and met Dominic. He came around to open my door, looking hot in leather and denim.

"You look good," he said as I hopped into the truck.

Self-consciously I pulled my jacket around myself. I was wearing my usual jeans and a comfortable blue T-shirt. I hadn't even taken the time to put on makeup or braid my hair. "I didn't do anything special."

"Yeah. That's what I like," he said with a faint smile.

And I liked how he looked, too, although I'd never say it out loud. His thick hair waved across thick dark brows and his smile softened his rugged features. I had this wild urge to move close to him, to lean against those hard muscles, to find out if his callused hands would be rough or soft. Crazy thoughts—and disloyal, too. I was happy with Josh—although right now he was probably dancing with other girls.

Dominic started the engine and I explained about wanting to go to the pavilion to contact Chloe and help her find peace. I hoped it wasn't a mistake to involve Dominic. I didn't believe Tawnya's paranoid story about Chloe. Ghosts couldn't physically harm humans. I was sure of this—almost.

Last night had been surreal, but tonight was a festival carnival complete with booths, food, entertainers, and even a band playing fifties music near the pavilion. Crowds of Chloe fans gathered for this final night of celebration. A dark cloudy sky hinted at rain, and the streets were so packed we had to park a mile away. As we entered the park, a costumed ghoul with a powdery face and black lipstick handed me a printed schedule of events.

"I've never been to a ghost party." Dominic rubbed his chin as he looked around.

"Wild, isn't it?"

"Weird is more like it."

"Yeah." I gestured toward the brochure. "Face-painting booths, a Freaks and Phantoms art exhibit, Poe and poetry readings, a talk about Chloe from some of her closest friends, a slide-show tour of the Chloe Museum, and club president Monique shares ghost-spotting techniques."

"Too many people and too much noise for me," Dominic said. "But Nona would love it."

"She would, wouldn't she? I wish she were here. I worry about her."

"Then call her. You can use my cell."

"I've made enough calls today." I thought of Josh and Penny-Love. "I'll call Nona when we have news about the remedy book. It's been missing for so long, I sure hope we can find it before Nona gets—well you know."

He nodded solemnly. "We'll find it," he assured.

I looked up at him, grateful for all his help and especially because he cared so much about my grandmother. "Thanks for driving me tonight."

"Why did you want to come? You can talk to ghosts anytime."

"Not Chloe," I said with a bitter laugh. "She doesn't play by the rules."

Then, because he was looking at me curiously and I owed him an explanation, I told him about my dream visions of Chloe. "I don't know what she wants, and she might even be dangerous. Tawyna sure thinks so."

"Tawyna?"

"The girl from the store." I felt a rush of satisfaction that he didn't even remember her name. "She told me a wild story about Chloe attacking her ex-boyfriend and warned me to keep a close watch on you."

"Sounds like fun," he said with a teasing look.

My cheeks warmed and I glanced at a middle-aged couple walking by holding hands and sporting matching dove temporary tattoos on their faces. Something like longing filled me, but I wasn't sure why. Uneasily, I turned back to Dominic.

"I don't believe Tawnya's story," I told him. "Chloe doesn't feel dangerous to me . . . just confused and lost."

"So you came to help her. That's cool."

"It's not like I had a choice. Chloe is one persistent ghost."

"Still you could have walked away. But you didn't and I admire that."

"Well . . ." The way he was staring at me made me a little dizzy. "It's my last chance to help her."

"What can I do?" Dominic offered.

"Driving me here was enough. I have to do the rest alone."

"I'll stay nearby if you need me," he said with sincerity.

"Just don't get too close to the cliff." I meant this as a joke, but neither of us laughed and chills rose on my skin.

While Dominic wandered over to the Freaks and Phantom art display, I wondered how to privately contact Chloe in the midst of all this crazy activity. The earlier connection I'd felt with her had faded. So I headed for her center of energy, the pavilion.

I hadn't gone far when I heard someone call my name. Turning around, I was surprised to see Cathy hurrying toward me. After dreaming of her and Chloe last night, it was jarring to see Cathy as an elderly woman. As a young girl, her rich auburn hair had been styled in a flip, very different from her wispy, fluffed, pink, cotton candy hair. Now she seemed much smaller, a withered shadow of the robust girl who loyally stood by Chloe.

"You aren't wearing a Chloe T-shirt," Cathy said with mischievous grin that gave me a glimpse of the young girl she used to be.

"Neither are you." I pointed at her sweater and slacks.

"Chloe won't mind." She laughed. "She'd love all this hoopla in her honor. She had such big dreams of being a star. But this isn't how they should have come true."

I nodded sympathetically, then glanced down at the printed schedule. "Are you one of the friends scheduled to talk about her?"

"Yes, and I'm so nervous about public speaking. I can't believe I let Monique rope me into this. Thank goodness Teddy came along with me for moral support."

"He's here?" I glanced around, but didn't see any sign of Chloe's former fiancé.

"He went to get us some sodas. I was surprised when he decided to join me. He usually avoids the celebration like poison."

"Will you mention him in your talk?"

"Heavens, no." She shook her head fervently. "He's a very private man and I would never embarrass him. I'll talk about the fun things Chloe and I did together."

"Do you expect to see her ghost?" I asked.

"No, although I'd love to," Cathy answered with a sigh. "I've attended every celebration but haven't even seen a ghostly glimmer. It hurts that Chloe shows herself to others, but not to me—her best friend. Maybe she blames me—"

In my dream, Cathy had started to tell Chloe something bad about James. My pulse quickened as I asked, "Blames you for what?"

"Oh, nothing." She looked away for a moment. "I was just talking silly."

"No, you weren't. You feel guilty." A vision popped into my head of young Cathy twirling a golden Hula-Hoop. She spun it on her arm until it grew smaller and smaller, until it was so tiny it twirled into a golden ring around her third finger.

"I don't have any reason to feel guilty," Cathy protested.

"What about the ring?"

The color drained from her face. "You can't possibly know! I only confided in two people. One I would trust with my life and the other is dead."

"Chloe. You told her about James and the ring," I added with the same knowing feeling I had whenever the phone rang and I just knew who it was.

With a nervous glance around, Cathy lowered her voice. "I only found out by accident. I was rushing to make an appointment, and literally bumped into him."

"James?" I asked.

"Yes. At first, I didn't recognize him. I'd only seen him a few times, but he was so different than local boys, with wavy golden hair and snazzy clothes. I was walking down the sidewalk, when bam! He ran into me and we both stumbled. I heard a ping and saw a gold band fall from his pocket."

"An engagement ring for Chloe?"

"You're half right. It was a wedding ring, but not for Chloe." Her eyes flamed furiously. "When

James grabbed it, I saw a pale indentation around his third finger where men usually wear wedding rings."

"*His ring?*" I gasped. "But that would mean James was—"

"A married man," she said with a solemn nod. "I didn't want to tell Chloe, but I had to stop her from making a terrible mistake—but it only made things worse. She was wild with anger. I never thought she'd still meet him that night. I don't know what happened—only that it ended with her death."

Something defensive in her tone made me suspicious. "Are you sure there wasn't more to it? No one ever heard from James again."

"He was probably afraid he'd be blamed for her death and ran away."

"Unless something happened to him."

"Ridiculous! He's most likely dead by now, and if not, he deserves to be."

Her cold tone made me shiver. Had James loved Chloe or had he killed her? And what had happened to him?

I gave Cathy a sharp look. "You said you told someone else about the ring."

"Well, yes. It was such a shock and I needed to talk, so I confided in someone I trusted."

"Who?"

She paused. "Teddy."

24

After Cathy left, I sat on a bench to sort through what I'd found out.

Everyone who knew Chloe gave a different picture of her. Which version was true? Was she a sweet and fun-loving girl or selfish and conniving? It was hard to know what to believe. Cathy's loyalty was shadowed with guilt. Teddy's devotion could hide dark secrets. Fan Club President Monique made Chloe sound as pure as a saint. And a man who never met Chloe created a museum in her honor. People were strange. No wonder Dominic preferred to work with animals.

Dominic appeared at my side as if my thoughts had conjured him. He cradled a small cottontail bunny in his arms. "Where'd you find him?" I asked as he sat beside me.

"Her," he corrected. "She was hiding under the Whizzer ride."

"Poor little thing," I said, reaching out to stroke her soft fur.

"She'll be fine once I take her home. Her family is beyond that fence, in those trees."

"Did she tell you that or is that a guess?"

"I never guess." He smiled, then invited me to walk with him. He held the bunny close to his chest, murmuring quietly to her. The bunny made a soft contented noise, like being next to Dominic was the coziest place on Earth.

Dominic went straight to a section of fencing, a small hole hidden by thick bushes. Kneeling down, he helped the small creature through the hole. When it hopped away, I imagined it reuniting with a loving family—no longer lost. That's what I wanted for Chloe, too.

Dominic stood, turning to me. "What are you thinking about?" he asked.

"Chloe."

"Seen any sign of her ghost yet?"

"Nope," I answered as we walked back to busy booths and noisy crowds. "I haven't even sensed her presence. It'll probably be stronger by the pavilion."

"If she does show up, what will you do?"

"Convince her to go to the other side. It won't be easy because she thinks James is still coming for her."

"He's a little late," Dominic said cynically.

"Maybe for a good reason. Like being dead. I'm beginning to suspect someone made sure he didn't meet Chloe that night."

"Can you use your powers to find out?"

"I don't have any real powers. But if my spirit guide were around, I could ask her." I swallowed hard, remembering how I'd told Opal to leave me alone. And she had.

"You really think someone killed James?"

"It's suspicious that no one ever saw him again."

"Any suspects?"

"Yeah." I nodded. "Chloe's fiancé."

Dominic gave a low whistle. "She had a fiancé and a boyfriend? That's asking for trouble."

"And she found it."

A sudden wind swirled leaves and the air sizzled as if charged with electricity. I tensed and looked around expectantly.

Dominic lightly touched my arm. "What is it?"

"I'm not sure . . . I sense something." I looked around, only seeing ordinary people enjoying a festival. No other-world visitors. Yet goose bumps prickled my skin and I sensed a storm of energy gathering around me.

The noise around me faded to a distant buzz and the world sharpened to bright, dizzying colors. Dominic's aura flamed with intense reds and oranges, and something inside me flamed, too. I thought of Josh surrounded by girls at the dance, and felt sad longing. I didn't want to be alone waiting on the sidelines.

A fifties band, set up on the raised pavilion, played a lively song. And for a moment, I had a dazzling vision of girls in full mid-skirts and guys with short haircuts. Dominic's blue eyes darkened and his craggy, rugged face softened so he reminded me of James. The James I'd danced with in a dream.

"The music is so lovely," I murmured.

"Do you know the song?"

"*Dance Away Love.*"

"I like it."

"You should. It's our song."

"When did we get a song?" He sounded amused. "Sabine, are you all right?"

"Never better." A wild urge to join the dancers filled me. Nothing seemed to matter, it was like dreaming while awake and I could hardly remember my own name. He'd called me Sabine, but that wasn't right.

"Why are we standing around?" I grabbed his hand. It was rougher than I expected, but still nice. "Let's dance."

"*You* want to dance with *me?*"

"I can't very well dance alone. Come on."

"Well, if you're sure."

"I'm sure," I said with confidence that surprised me.

It was as if the pavilion was a stage and we were actors taking our places into familiar roles. As his fingers curled snugly around mine and he pulled me close, a rational part of my brain screamed, "What are you doing?" But another part shut out the questions and surrendered to the music.

There were other couples on the pavilion, but I was barely aware of them. With golden lights shining down, soft as sunshine, I leaned against my dance partner and floated away. Swaying in perfect rhythm, we danced as if we'd done this a hundred times before. And it felt right.

"You're a good dancer," I murmured dreamily.

"So are you."

"I live for dancing."

"You do?" he asked. "I didn't know that."

"Now you do." A strand of my hair flew across my eyes and I stared at the pale color in confusion. It should be darker, a rich shade of caramel. And why was I wearing jeans at a public dance? My parents would be shocked.

"You're different tonight," he told me.

"Different in a good way, I hope." I flashed him a teasing look. "It's my number-two goal in life to keep everyone guessing."

"And what's number one?"

"To achieve great things. I'm going to be famous."

"Famous?" he repeated with a puzzled tilt of his head. "Since when did you care about that?"

"Always! My dreams are bigger than a thousand pavilions."

"I hope they come true."

"They're starting to," I said, my heart soaring as I met his gaze. "Finding the right person to share your dreams is important. No one really took me seriously before, but it's all going to change soon. Everything will be perfect after you take me away."

"You want to leave already?"

"Not the dance, silly." Impatience and a powerful longing rose in my soul. Why was he looking at me so strangely? "I want to go places. Not tied down to Teddy—"

"Teddy?" He knitted his brows. "Who's he?"

His question threw me off balance, and my world tilted as if I was slipping over a sharp edge.

Dancers whirled by in a blur, spinning faster, faster. I tried to remember what I was doing here. But the memory seemed distant and my mind drifted along while the band played. There were no worries or cages of rules on the dance floor. Only music.

"I wish the song would never end," I murmured, enjoying the warm comfort of my cheek pressed against his shoulder.

"Everything has to end eventually."

"Not for us. It's only beginning."

"Are you okay Sabine?"

"You're teasing again. You know that's not my name."

He gave me a strange look. "I do?"

"Don't say anything more." I grabbed for him, holding tight to dreams, I whispered desperately, "Just dance."

He nodded, saying nothing at all.

We drifted away from other dancers, to a secluded corner of the pavilion. Fears faded to a peaceful sense of joy. Everything was going to be all right. I was young, talented, and powerful. I could do anything, go anywhere, achieve everything, and no one could stop me.

Thunder rumbled nearby, but it was safe and protected under the pavilion, where dancers whirled and voices lifted in laughter. My heart lifted, too. And when I looked up into the most handsome face in the world, I knew he was the only one for me. My fairy-tale prince coming to the rescue.

"James, my love," I said softly as I circled my arms around his neck.

He shook his head, yet didn't pull away. His eyes shone brightly, more sky blue than night black. And his golden hair seemed unusually dark.

Lightning flashed as we stood alone in our own universe. His gaze smoldered. Hot, intense, wanting—my breath came faster, warmth flowing through me. I parted my lips and lifted my chin. He hesitated for only a moment, then brought his lips hungrily down on my own. The hands pulling me close were oddly rough, yet amazingly soft. Our hearts pounded a wild rhythm and I tasted salty desire on his lips.

Rain fell around the pavilion.

And we kissed.

25

I was floating in a wonderful dream where someone loved me and I loved him in return. There was music and happiness and no problems. I longed to live in this moment forever. From far away, I heard someone calling.

Sabine . . . Sabine. . . .

That name again! I thought with irritation. Energy surged then faded. A jolt of clarity rocked my mind—and I was back. It was like waking suddenly from a dream. I blinked fast, panic rising inside me. What had just happened? Why was I kissing Dominic?

Jumping back, I stared at Dominic in shock. He looked confused and reached for me, but I backed further away. "Is something wrong?" he asked.

"Everything!" I choked out. "How could you? I can't believe I was just—that we were—"

"Kissing?" Dominic smiled.

"Ohmygod!"

"Is that a compliment or complaint?"

"You don't understand—it wasn't me! It was . . . HER!"

He frowned, looking a bit dazed, too. I wanted to explain, but all I could do was sputter and shake my head. How could I blame what just happened on a ghost? That was crazy—even for me!

Turning around, I ran. I was hardly aware of the rain as I jumped off the pavilion, only shame and embarrassment. I had to get away.

It wasn't my fault, I tried to reassure myself as I dodged around a group of children waving balloons. It was Chloe. She loved to dance, not me. All the romantic desires were hers, not mine. She started the kiss with James—yet I'd finished it with Dominic. And heaven help me, I'd enjoyed it.

"Sabine, wait!"

Ignoring Dominic, I ran faster, racing past booths, only slowing once to avoid an old guy in a ghoul costume. Then I sprinted through the gate and out of the park. Tightening my jacket against the rain, I had no destination in mind except far away.

But there was no running from my shame. Over and over, I kept replaying the kiss. Not sweet and friendly like my kisses with Josh, but wild and powerful. I hadn't known it was possible.

Oh, Josh! I'm so sorry, I thought guiltily. I'd worried about him cheating on me with other girls, yet I was the betrayer. How could I explain it to him? Josh would never believe I'd been possessed by a ghost. But that was the truth—it had been Chloe. Not content to invade my dreams, she'd taken over my body. Yet I'd been there, too, sharing wild emotions, enjoying myself. . . .

I ran even faster, passing the cemetery and into the main section of town. I recognized stores and hurried up on the sidewalk to escape the rain. Had it only been this afternoon that I'd been here with Thorn and Dominic? That seemed like another lifetime. How could I ever talk to Dominic again? What did he think of me? Or had a ghost possessed him, too?

I was out of breath and my jacket was drenched. Shaking my wet hair, I took refuge under the barbershop awning and sat on a bench. Wrapping my arms around myself, I tried to keep my body from shaking.

I don't know how long I sat there. It may have only been minutes, but it felt like decades. When my heart slowed and I felt almost normal again, I had to face the fact that running away didn't solve anything. I had to talk to Dominic. He'd been under Chloe's spell, too, or he never would have kissed me. So he'd have to understand. He was probably embarrassed, too, and would be happy to forget it ever happened.

Resolved, I stood up from the bench.

But as I stepped out into the street, the storm lashed out full force and rain pounded so fiercely I ran for cover. When I looked up, I realized I stood on the threshold of the Chloe Museum. It seemed more than coincidence.

I was beyond surprise when I found the door unlocked. The sound of rain faded as I entered the building. The air was still with a faint aroma of vanilla. This was my chance to find out what secrets were hidden behind the red-heart door.

Water dripped from my hair and clothes as I cautiously entered the museum. I shivered slightly, more from facing the unknown than the cold. And when I reached the forbidden door with its bright red heart, the knob turned easily—as if it were inviting me to enter.

My eyes adjusted to the dim lighting, and I saw that the room wasn't much larger than a closet. It was lined with glass cases and framed news clippings on the wall. Finding a wall switch, I flipped it on. Only instead of flooding the room with light, haunting music flowed from hidden speakers. The same melody I'd heard in my dreams.

Chloe's song.

I strained my eyes to study the news clippings. Yellow with age and bold headlines: "Local Girl's Tragic Fall, Dancing Leads to Death" and "Missing

Young Man Still Sought." This was the first evidence that hinted at James's involvement in Chloe's death. I skimmed the article, but there was little information about him. No one knew his full name or where he came from. But I did find out more details about Chloe's death. The rain-soaked dirt at the cliff's edge had crumbled beneath her and she'd plunged down a steep canyon. It wasn't the fall that killed her, but a dead tree with a sharp branch. She'd literally died of a broken heart.

There were pictures, too. Icy prickles rose on my skin as I looked at the smiling girl, her full skirt spinning as she danced on her last day of life. And there in the background, close behind her, was a handsome golden haired young man. His smile hinted at smugness and his dark eyes were bold and confident.

James. It was as if I knew him intimately—how sweet words slid so easily from his soft lips, his warm, eager touch, and how he laughed easily at jokes, especially his own.

My cheeks warmed and I quickly turned my attention to the glass cases. They were filled with odd items: bits of torn clothing, scattered pearls, a scrap of nylon, a hairbrush, and a ring missing a stone—the sort of things you'd find in someone's garbage, not protected under glass.

An invisible force drew me to a small glass case half-hidden in a corner. When I saw the object inside, I choked back horror. It was a sharp branch, twisted and darkened with odd patches. And I realized why this room was forbidden.

Instead of celebrating Chloe's life, it showcased her death. Broken jewelry, tattered clothes, bloodstains, and a branch from the tree that ended her life.

But why would Kasper, a man who never even knew Chloe, create such a sick collection? Was he some kind of pervert? Or was there another, darker reason?

And then it hit me.

I turned back to the picture of Chloe and James. And I looked at it, staring deep into faces. Take away the golden hair, add age lines and about fifty pounds, and the resemblance was unmistakable. And shocking.

So many things suddenly made sense: Chloe's ghost started making annual appearances nine years ago—about the same time Kasper moved to town, Kasper's odd obsession with a girl who died a half-century ago began, and Chloe's insistence that James was still here—because he was.

Only he'd changed his name to Kasper.

26

I was so stunned, I wasn't aware that someone had crept up behind me—until a rough hand grabbed my shoulder and spun me around.

"What do think you're doing in here? I told you to stay away!" Kasper's fleshy face flamed with fury.

"James!" I exclaimed, then slapped my hand over my mouth.

"What did you . . . YOU!" He glared at me with intense hatred. "You've been poking around too much."

I backed up against a wall, still reeling from this realization. Now that I studied him close up, it was so obvious. The good looks had faded, but the cocky attitude was still etched in hard lines around his mouth and forehead.

"You should have left when I warned you," he said harshly.

"You! You left the note and made that phone call! But how did you know about my grandmother?"

"You used a credit card in my store. It only took a quick credit check to find out about you."

"But why me? I never did anything to you."

"Not me—Chloe. I had to stop you from sending her away. I've dealt with your kind before."

"My kind!"

"I've studied enough freaks to recognize one when I see one. You weren't the first psychic to come here. I got rid of them and I'll get rid of you, too."

"What do you mean?" I cried, so flat against the wall now that I could feel the rough wood stabbing into my shoulder.

"I've had my fill of nosy psychics, claiming to see ghosts and knowing more about Chloe than I do. It doesn't matter that I never see her ghost myself. I know she's there every October when other people see her. She's my ghost and no one's gonna send her away. I got a good thing here with this museum and my books. You're not going to ruin it."

He reached out viciously for my arm, and jerked me out of the room. For an old guy, he was surprisingly strong. I struggled, but it was no use. He kicked the red-heart door shut and pulled me down the hall. I could hardly breathe. My mind raced, grasping this new horror. I kicked out and connected with soft flesh. He grunted with pain, but didn't let go. With a furious snarl, he wrenched my arm back so hard I screamed

"Shut up!" he barked.

"That hurts! Let go!" Pricks of light in blackness swam before my eyes.

He shoved me forward.

I stumbled and would have fallen except he jerked me to my feet. My arms felt as if they were breaking and tears stung my eyes. The more I struggled, the sharper the pain. I wondered where he was taking me, terrified to find out. Was he going to kill me—or worse?

He stopped in front of a door, yanked it open, and flung me forward. "In there."

My arms flailed and I stumbled, falling, bumping down a staircase, landing painfully on a hard floor. A door slammed from above and a bolt locked.

Feeling my way back up the stairs, I found the door and shook the knob. Rattling, pulling, and screaming to be let out until my voice grew hoarse. Finally, I gave up and I sank wearily onto the top step.

Trapped.

I'd been stuck in a room at school once, and while that had been scary, at least I knew I'd get out eventually. There was no knowing anything now—except fear.

Trembling, I called out with my mind. "Opal, I need you."

I listened, waited, desperate to hear her comforting voice.

"Please, Opal. I need your help."

But there was no answer. And I felt abandoned. How could she let me down when I needed her the most?

Then I thought of all the people I'd let down lately—Penny-Love, Josh, Thorn, my sisters. And I hadn't succeeded in helping Nona, either. I hadn't meant to hurt anyone, yet I had. And now that I needed help, there was no one around. My actions were coming full circle. Karma, Nona would call it.

Time drifted to a kind of numb blur as I huddled on the stair step. After a while my eyes adjusted, and I made out bulky shapes. Stacked boxes, a broken bicycle, a legless chair, a lopsided couch, a ripped mattress, a folded Ping-Pong table, and even a juke box.

I guessed I was in the museum's basement.

What did Kasper have planned for me? I should have fought harder and ran away when I'd had the chance. But he seemed so old and harmless, like a nerdy Santa Claus. But there was nothing jolly about keeping gruesome momentos of

Chloe's death. Had he bought or stolen them from a police evidence room? He was totally twisted.

I thought back to our first meeting at the museum. On my way out, I'd told him the phone was going to ring *before* it rang. At the time it seemed like a harmless trick. But now I realized I'd given myself away. He'd seen me at the park last night talking with Chloe and must have switched on the pavilion lights. He would have been desperate to get rid of me before I got rid of Chloe. He faked the phone call saying my grandmother was in the hospital. When that didn't work, he'd probably seen the yellow jeep drive by and followed us out to Peaceful Pines and left the warning note.

It all made terrifying sense. But what would happen when he returned? He couldn't let me go—not now.

I have to get out of here before he comes back!

Jumping up, I pounded desperately on the door. But it was locked and built so sturdily that I'd need something heavy to break through. And the lock wasn't one of those old, easy-to-pick types. This one was gleaming brass, state of the art, and undoubtedly bolted. The only way to open it was from the other side with a key. And the only windows were too high and small to work.

Still, I couldn't just give up. So I explored the room, searching for anything that might help me escape. I moved boxes, peered into dark corners, and crawled behind heavy furniture. But all I found were cobwebs and solid brick walls. After bumping my sore knee again, I sank down on the floor in defeat.

Hopeless.

I looked at my watch—11:20. I'd been here for nearly an hour. What was happening at the celebration? Had Cathy given her speech? Had the guest of honor made an appearance? Was Kasper watching with satisfied delight? And what about Dominic? Had he given up on me and returned to his campsite?

I closed my eyes and concentrated hard again on Opal. She was supposed to watch over me, so where was she? More than anything I longed to hear her comforting voice. She wouldn't just let me rot here—not unless I was meant to be like Chloe. Was it my destiny to die young?

Shuddering, I wrapped my arms around my shoulders. A draft of air swirled around my ankles. And I sensed something different.

Opening my eyes, I saw a glowing silver globe floating in the air, rising high over my head.

"Who are you?" I whispered. "Opal?"

The light glowed brighter, taller, and wider. It shimmered into a misty shape of a young girl with flowing caramel hair and a full cotton skirt.

Chloe was back.

27

"I've never been so glad to see a ghost!"

She smiled faintly, her form translucent and hard to make out, as she had less energy away from the pavilion. I wasn't sure if I could trust her—she had just possessed my body a short while ago. But I sensed she was on my side and wanted to help.

"Get me out of here!" I said anxiously.

She lifted her hand and pointed toward a dark, dusty corner of the basement where boxes were stacked nearly to the ceiling.

"What do you mean? Do you want me to look in the boxes?"

With a shake of her head, she floated up and over the boxes. She crooked her finger, gesturing for me follow—so I did.

She ducked behind the boxes, then popped back up, motioning for me to come with her. While I moved the boxes aside, she hovered overhead. I could see a dusty hole behind the boxes. Her glow showered light so I could see clearly. There were more boxes, but these were smaller and easier for me to move aside. When I was done, I found myself facing a wood-paneled wall.

"Now what?" I cried anxiously.

Chloe swept over to the wall and then vanished.

"Come back!" I called, reaching out and touching the wood.

When the wood wobbled, I realized it wasn't solid, but a large sheet of plywood propped against the wall. I shoved it aside and glimpsed a shadowy face. My scream cut off when I recognized the face—my own! Light from outside reflected my own image in a grimy window.

The latch on the window had been broken a long time ago. Had this been Chloe's escape route? Now over fifty years later, it was my escape route, too.

After tugging and banging on the window, I pried it open. Cold, rainy air rushed in and I gasped with relief. I quickly scrambled through the window and found myself in a narrow alley.

Now which way? I wondered, pushing my damp hair from my face. The rain had eased to sprinkles, but I was still soggy and cold. I stood there, unsure which way to go—until I saw a glowing shape to my right like a ghostly beacon offering guidance.

This narrow passage ended at the sidewalk. Hearing the sound of a door closing, I looked at the museum entrance and covered my mouth so I wouldn't scream. A chubby bald man was stepping out of the door. I gasped.

He whirled toward me and shouted, "YOU!"

Blood pulsed through me and gave life with fear. When I stared to run, I heard him yell for me to stop. But I kept running, following a glowing light that I knew was Chloe. Everything blurred as I moved, but instead of heading back for the celebration, I turned up a hilly trail, higher and higher. I didn't hear Kasper behind me and hoped I'd lost him.

I slowed at the top of the hill, startled to find myself in a familiar rocky clearing. I heard clomping footsteps and turned back to see Kasper. His face blazed with rage, and he lifted his hands to aim a gun at me.

He was totally insane and I was going to be totally dead. Ohmygod! I knew I was going to die. This was my fate, like Chloe's. Only no one would celebrate my death, few would even mourn me. No! I couldn't just give up. There had to be a way out, but what? I was trapped between a cliff and a killer.

Then something in the air changed; energy shimmered like a glowing tornado. The glow slowed and settled into a ghostly shape.

"Chloe!" I screamed. "Help! Stop James!"

James? she whispered in a tone haunted with pain. But her expression was confused and I realized she didn't recognize Kasper. It made sense, I suppose, since he'd changed so much, while Chloe had stayed the same.

Shivering, I glanced at Kasper. The gun fell from his hand and he stared at Chloe. "I can see you!" he cried in shock. "After all these years—I never saw you before—I was never completely sure. . ." His words trailed off and his face went as pale as death.

The other times Chloe appeared she was misty and hard to see. But being here, in the place of her death, made her glow with blinding energy. She shimmered so bright my eyes ached. But I couldn't turn away, caught up in her powerful emotions.

She hovered high off the ground, dry grass swayed in her wind and bits of twigs and rocks skittered across my feet. I didn't move as something even more amazing happened. As I watched Kasper-James, he changed. He grew taller, his wrinkled face smoothed, softening, and his saggy flesh thinned, and golden hair spread across his bald head. The illusion only lasted for a moment.

James. Chloe reached shimmering fingers towards him. *I've been waiting.*

"Don't hurt me! Stay away!" His eyes widened with fear. "It wasn't my fault."

She hovered on the air, her essence so bright my eyes stung. *Why did you leave me? I waited . . . so lonely.*

"It was an accident. You were angry, shouting that I had betrayed you, then rushing at me so fast, I jumped aside and you fell. I didn't mean for you to die—and I was so scared. I knew they'd blame me."

"You did betray her," I said, accusing. "You can't hide from her anymore. But you can help me show her how to find peace on the other side."

He ignored me, putting his hands in front of his face protectively as he backed up. "Don't hurt me—keep away!"

But Chloe swirled closer, a brilliant glowing vision. *James–don't leave me–come to me.* Her silvery shape glistened like tears. Caramel hair flowed around her like dark rain as she reached for James.

"Keep away!" he ordered, turning to run.

But quick as lightning, she flashed past me to block his way. Electricity crackled, sparking around Chloe, until her essence shone as fiery as a burning sunset.

I waited and waited, Chloe murmured. *For you.*

She swept ominously closer to him. I struggled to find the words to help her, to free her of her pain and help her find peace on the other side. But things happened too fast.

Chloe kept coming after James. He backed up, and would have collided with me if I hadn't flung myself sideways. I landed hard on the muddy ground. My head hit something hard, a bush or log, and for a moment I laid there dazed.

When my head cleared and I wiped mud from my eyes, I saw Chloe and James close to the cliff. Misty rain swirled with Chloe as she advanced toward James. His face paled with terror and he didn't seem to realize he was backing closer to the edge.

"Watch out!" I shouted to him.

But he didn't seem to hear and stepped back blindly. Slipping, stumbling, his arms flailing in the air as he disappeared. His hollow scream seemed to echo forever.

Chloe hovered in the air over the cliff, her essence fading until I could only see a faint shimmer of caramel brown. I heard her murmur, *Wait for me, James.*

28

"So Kasper was actually James? And he went crazy with grief and fell off the cliff? That's so tragic! And to think I slept through it all!" Thorn exclaimed the next morning as I folded clothes into my suitcase. It had been past midnight when I returned last night. I'd been too stunned to talk, leaving the tragedy for others to sort out, numb as Dominic led me away.

I hadn't wanted to leave, but Dominic insisted. "There's no good to come from telling the truth." And I knew he was right. Kasper—AKA—James was beyond my help.

"It all seems like a bad dream," I now admitted to Thorn.

"At least they're together," Thorn said, sitting cross-legged on her unmade bed.

"Yeah. Chloe got what she wanted." I sighed, sadness mingled with closure. I sensed that finally–fifty-four years after her death—Chloe was at peace.

"So I guess this will end the Chloe Celebrations," Thorn was saying. "My aunt will be glad. But there's something she won't be happy about."

"What?" I shut my suitcase and eyed her curiously.

"I've decided to fess up. It's time I let her see the real me."

"Are you sure?"

"Totally." Thorn pulled out a plastic makeup bag and black wig from her suitcase. "Watch out world, Thorn is back. My aunt will have to get used to the real me."

"Great!" I applauded, then added with a wistful sigh, "If only I had your courage. Then I'd stand up to my mother and tell her I'm going to my sisters' birthday party whether she likes it or not."

"You survived a lot last night," Thorn said as she slipped on dagger-shaped earrings. "I am so glad I don't see ghosts. I think you're like the bravest person I know."

For the first time that morning, I smiled. Maybe I was brave when I had to be. I couldn't run from my problems—including my mother.

*　　*　　*

A half-hour later, I was hanging up the phone when Thorn came back with the widest smile I'd ever seen on her face. "You're never gonna guess what my aunt said when she saw me!"

I imagined what an old-fashioned woman would think of Thorn's pale, striking black-and-white makeup, black leather, and multiple piercings. "Did she scream?" I asked.

"No. She just asked what I wanted for breakfast."

"No way!"

"Not one word about my black hair and Goth look. When I asked why she wasn't surprised, she said that she already knew. Apparently my mother showed her pictures. And Aunt Deb never even let on."

"Well that's good, isn't it? She doesn't mind and you don't have to be fake."

"Yeah—and that's not all," Thorn added. "Aunt Deb rolled down her waistband and showed me her pierced belly button."

"Pierced!" I choked out in delight.

"With a tiny diamond. She said that even middle-aged ladies like to rebel a little."

"So next she'll be going Goth, too," I teased.

"I hope not, that would be too weird." Thorn glanced at the phone and asked more seriously, "So how did the call to your mom go?"

"Okay. I guess." I kept my expression calm, although inside I was still intimidated and anxious. "Mom isn't happy, but that's her problem. I'm going to the party so my sisters won't be disappointed. I'm doing this for Amy and Ashley."

"Good for you," she said with a pat on my shoulder. I just nodded, knowing that I still had a battle ahead with my mother. But I'd deal with that later.

French toast was delicious, and it was cool to have the real Thorn back.

While we were washing and drying dishes afterward, there was a sharp honk from outside. Thorn raced to the front window and peered out. Following her, I saw a bright yellow jeep pulling in the driveway.

"My jeep!" she cried joyously, then tossed her washrag down and sped outside.

Another vehicle pulled in behind the jeep—Dominic's battered white truck. Goat, Dominic's mechanic friend stepped out of the jeep and handed over the keys to Thorn.

The jeep gleamed like new. Thorn caressed her hand over the smooth canvas, and I was pleased that you couldn't even tell where it had been punctured.

After Thorn hugged and thanked Dominic, she asked him if he would drive me out to Peaceful Pines since she wanted to spend more time with her aunt. Dominic gave me an uncertain look. "As long as Sabine is okay with it," he said cautiously.

"Sounds great," I said, surprised at how much the idea of going with him pleased me. Of course, that's just because he'd been so much help and I knew he cared about Nona. It had nothing to do with the kiss. He hadn't mentioned it, and neither had I—as if we'd silently agreed to pretend it never happened. We were friends, nothing more. And I needed all the friends I could get. My life was sure to change soon—and not in a good way. Evan was probably already planning his revenge.

Dominic dropped his friend off at the auto shop, then we drove through Pine Peaks on our way to Peaceful Pines Resort. As we passed the heart of town, I asked Dominic to slow down. Then I stared with a heavy heart at the Chloe Museum. The curtains were drawn, there were no lights, and on the door was a large CLOSED sign.

Dominic glanced at me curiously, but said nothing, and I was grateful. Being so close to him made me self-conscious. Like I wondered if my hair was messy or if my makeup was bad or if my jeans fit right. I looked down at my lap and realized I was wringing my hands. To give my hands something to do, I asked Dominic to borrow his phone so I could call Nona.

Only it wasn't Nona who answered. Penny-Love was there, helping with the love business again. I braced myself, feeling bad for letting her down with the dance. But instead of chewing me out, she was excited about a new guy she met while setting up decorations, he was from the art club and volunteered to help out at the last minute.

"So thanks to you, I have a new guy!"

I told her it was great, and fought the urge to ask about Josh. I knew Penny-Love would tell me exactly what he did at the dance. But I found myself reluctant to know. As if suspecting him of dancing with other girls made me feel less guilty.

Still there was one thing I had to know. "Was Evan at the dance?" I asked.

"Evan Marshall? Sure, he was there. He had a new girlfriend, too, kind of skinny with bad teeth. I didn't talk to her, but heard she was from San Jose. Isn't that where your family lives? Maybe you know her?"

"No!" I said too sharply. "It's a huge city."

"Yeah, I figured that."

"So did Evan say anything odd . . ." I hesitated, "About me?"

"No. Why would he or anyone else? You're like the most normal person I know."

She laughed, and after swallowing the lump in my throat, I laughed, too.

My reputation was safe . . .for now.

Minutes later, we arrived in Peaceful Pines Retirement Resort.

As we stepped out of the truck, I noticed an elderly couple heading towards a white sedan. I was surprised to recognize Teddy and Cathy, dressed in formal clothes, their arms linked cozily. When Cathy spotted me, she rushed over to give me a hug.

"Thank you, dear," she whispered.

"For what?" I asked.

"For getting that old fool to face the past instead of pretending it never happened." She tilted her head toward Teddy who waited by the sedan. "Last night he took me to the celebration and this morning he's invited me to church."

"But all we did was talk about Chloe."

"Which he hasn't done for over fifty years. I think he's finally forgiven Chloe—and me. When he held my hand, I got all funny inside like I was sixteen again. Who knows? We might even go steady." She giggled, then waved and hurried back to Teddy.

Dominic was giving me a curious look. "What was that about?"

"Young love," I told him with a smile. "They make a cute couple, don't you think?"

He arched his brows, clearly not sure if I was teasing or serious, and that was fine with me. Then we entered the resort and made our way to Eleanor Baskers's cottage.

And this time when I knocked, the door opened. A friendly-looking woman with thick blue-framed glasses and a colorful tiny braid woven in her medium-length brown hair stood there. When she smiled, I noticed a gap in her front teeth.

Her eyes widened and she exclaimed. "You!"

I looked around, wondering if someone was standing behind me. But her gaze fixed on me, leaving no doubt I was the object of her surprise.

"Uh . . . do you know me?"

"Not yet, but I've been expecting you," she said mysteriously. Without even asking our names or what we were doing there, she ushered us inside her home.

The first thing I noticed about her warm home were the cows. Hundreds, maybe thousands, of glass, porcelain, stuffed, wood, and plastic cows filed on shelves. There was even a cow-shaped coffee table. And when I sat on a black-and-white couch, my elbow brushed against a pillow that mooed.

"After we talk, I'll take you on the complete tour of my collection," she told us with a proud smile. "I have a case of Elsie memorabilia in a back room, including several purple cows like that old poem."

"Poem?" I repeated.

But Dominic nodded and quoted, "I never saw a purple cow, I never hope to see one, but I can tell you anyhow—"

"I'd rather see than be one!" Eleanor chimed in, laughing. "How in the world did you know that old poem?"

"He reads a lot," I said wryly. "Practically lives at the library."

Eleanor smiled approvingly, then she sat down in a chair across from the couch and grew serious. "Now we need to discuss my dream."

"Your dream?" I questioned.

"Last night I had the most bizarre dream, and you were in it."

"But you don't even know me."

"That's what makes it so unusual. A woman with thick black hair and rather exotic features, like she was Egyptian or Indian, was sitting on the edge of my bed. It felt more real than any dream I've ever had before."

"Opal," I whispered, warmed inside. She hadn't deserted me after all.

"Yes, Opal. That's what she called herself. She held a photo album and opened it to show me pictures of a young blond girl."

"Me?"

"Yes." Eleanor nodded. "And she told me to expect you today. I thought it was a weird dream until I opened my door just now."

"What else did she say?" I asked eagerly.

"That I was to tell you a story about my great-grandmother. I'd almost forgotten the story, but now it's crystal clear in my mind. About how my great-grandmother Martha took in four neighbor girls when their mother died. She wanted to raise the girls and keep them together, but they were taken from her and adopted separately."

"Agnes and her daughters!" My pulse quickened. "That's what I came to find out. Agnes was my ancestor and it's urgent I find a family book of remedies that's been lost for a long time. Do you know anything about it?"

She shook her head. "Sorry, but I don't."

"What about the sisters? Any idea what happened to them?"

"Now there I can help you." Mrs. Baskers scooted her chair closer. "About a year after the girls were sent away, Martha had a knock at her door, and there stood a dour-faced woman with a small girl. The little girl was the youngest of the four sisters, and the family who'd taken her didn't want her anymore."

"The poor girl. What happened?"

"She stayed." Eleanor smiled. "And grew up to become my grandmother."

"So you're—we're related?" I jumped, almost knocking over a cow-shaped coat rack.

"Very distant cousins. I'm afraid I can't tell you much about our mutual relatives. The four sisters weren't ever reunited."

I sighed, my hopes sinking.

"But I have a record of their adopted names. After my dream, I searched out the records and wrote the names down." She pulled out a small paper from the pocket of her skirt and handed it to me.

Dominic was watching quietly, taking this all in, not saying anything but his blue eyes shone with interest.

"Wow!" I exclaimed, only glancing at the names. Impulsively, I gave my new distant cousin a hug. "Thank you so much!"

"You're very welcome. The woman in my dream asked me to give you something else." She stood up and walked over to a fireplace mantel. Pushing aside a glass statue of a cow jumping over a moon, she lifted up a small envelope. Then she returned and handed the envelope to me.

"I don't understand what this is about, but I understand about family and love, and I want to help." She handed the envelope to me. "This has been in my family for a very long time, and now I'm happy to pass it on to you."

Hardly able to breathe, I lifted open the envelope flap.

I pulled out a tiny silver charm shaped like an old-fashioned house.

My second charm! I was halfway towards finding the remedy book. I couldn't wait to tell Nona!

"Since we're cousins, I've decided to give you something else," Mrs. Baskers added with a mysterious smile. "I found it when I was rummaging around in the attic, and frankly I had no idea what to do with it. Until now."

"What is it?"

"An object of superstition," she said with a wink as if she didn't take superstitions seriously. "It was used to ward off evil spirits. All it's been doing in my attic is gathering dust. With a little polishing, it will make a lovely decoration."

I stared in awe at the reflective mirror-like sphere. I'd never seen one before, but Nona had told me stories about these magical objects. When I touched the sphere, I had a strong feeling the stories were true. And that something ancient still lurked inside.

"Do you know what it is?" the old woman asked me.

"Yes." I shivered. "A witch ball.

The End

THE SEER

Look for
The seer, volume 3
witch ball

*   *   *

**Check out other books from
Llewellyn Publications.
Visit www.llewellyn.com**

check out these new books
from Llewellyn

"I know your secret . . ."

Stacey Brown is not the most popular junior girl at Hillcrest boarding school, or the prettiest, or the smartest. She has confidence issues, a crush on the boyfriend of her best friend, Drea, and she has painful secrets. Oh yeah, Stacy is also a hereditary witch. Now, she's having nightmares that someone is out to murder Drea.

Stacey has a history with dreams and murder—one she doesn't want to repeat. She's determined to use her skills to find the killer before the killer finds Drea. Edgy and engaging, Laurie Faria Stolarz takes her readers on an unforgettable ride with this witchy thriller.

0-7387-0391-5

288 pages $8.95

"I'm watching you . . ."

One year later. It's happening again. Seventeen-year-old Stacey Brown is having nightmares.

Stacey really should be focusing on getting into college—not to mention the rocky path her love life has been taking lately. But even if she could ignore the dreams, Stacey can't ignore the strange letters she's been receiving. No address, no signature—and the same cryptic messages she's been hearing in her nightmares.

What's worse is that she's not the only one having weird dreams. Jacob, a transfer student, says he's been dreaming of Stacey's death for months, dreams so realistic that he transferred schools to save her—or so he says. If that weren't enough, Stacey's starting to have feelings for him, even though she already has a boyfriend. But can she trust Jacob? Or will both their darkest dreams come true?

0-7387-0443-1

312 pages $8.95

"I'll make you pay . . . "

School's out, and Stacey and company have hit the beach for one last glorious summer of freedom before college.

There's just one little catch, though. Nightmares again. Stacey and Jacob are both having dreams. Stacey keeps seeing the death of Clara, an oddly familiar fifteen-year-old staying in a cabin nearby. Stacey is determined not to let her nightmares about Clara come true and wants everyone's help. Jacob isn't talking about his dreams, though, and secrets are starting to take a toll on their relationship.

Add to this mix a rocky start to the summer for Chad and Drea, fireworks from PJ and Amber, revenge, frat boys, and shocking final twist, and Laurie Stolarz has done it again.

0-7387-0631-0

288 pages $8.95

"The boy was pleasing, if you like that desperate look . . . Too bad I might have to kill him."

A fun summer roadtrip and a much-needed break from his nagging dad takes a fantastic turn when seventeen-year-old Bren stops in Live Oak Springs Township in search of a bathroom.

Suddenly, Bren is dragged onto the Path of Shadows by Jasmina "Jazz" Corey, Queen of the Witches (who is, as it happens, drop-dead gorgeous and Bren's age). Bren finds himself in a world of witches, hags, sirens, and slithers. It is also a world in danger of total annihilation at the hands of an ancient evil.

Bren and Jazz are the only ones who can fight the evil Shadowmaster and save witches and humans alike—if they can stop fighting with each other.

0-7387-0561-6

312 pages $9.95

Don't miss the first book in The Seer series.

After getting kicked out of school and sent to live with her grandmother, Sabine Rose is determined to become a "normal" teenage girl. She hides her psychic powers from everyone, even from her grandmother Nona, who also has "the gift." Having a job at the school newspaper and friends like Penny-Love, a popular cheerleader, have helped Sabine fit in at her new school. She has even managed to catch the eye of the adorable Josh DeMarco.

Yet, Sabine can't seem to get the bossy voice of Opal, her spirit guide, out of her head . . . or the disturbing images of a girl with a dragonfly tattoo. Suspected of a crime she didn't commit, Sabine must find the strength to defend herself and later save a friend from certain danger.

0-7387-0526-8

288 pages

$6.99

A fun introduction to the Tarot—just for young adults.

Teens who want to discover and unlock their psychic abilities will find no better guide than Maria Shaw, who has a knack for making New Age topics exciting to teens.

Maria covers all the basics, from a smattering of history to in-depth descriptions of all the cards. Common concerns such as how to prepare for a reading, how to cut the cards, how to ask questions, and how to choose the best days for readings are discussed in detail. Sixteen different card spreads, including teen love layouts, the guardian angel/spirit guide spread, and the big question spread, give new readers lots of options.

The book includes a deck of Tarot cards.

0-7387-0523-3

192 pages   **$19.95**

To write to the author

If you wish to contact the author, please write to the author in care of Llewellyn Worldwide, and we will forward your letter. Both the author and publisher appreciate hearing from you and learning of your enjoyment of this book. Llewellyn Worldwide cannot guarantee that every letter written to the author can be answered, but all will be forwarded. Please write to:

Linda Joy Singleton
⁄ Llewellyn Worldwide
2143 Wooddale Drive, Dept. 0-7387-0526-8
Woodbury, MN 55125-2989

Please enclose a self-addressed stamped envelope, or one dollar to cover costs. If outside U.S.A., enclose international postal reply coupon.

Many of Llewellyn's authors have Web sites with additional information and resources. For more information, please visit our Web site at:

http://www.llewellyn.com

Llewellyn Worldwide does not participate in, endorse, or have any authority or responsibility concerning private business transactions between our authors and the public.